All in a Girl's Best Interest

To Address Sex.

Josiah Hutchison

All characters, places, and allusions named herein are of fictional origin and are intended exclusively for the entertainment of the reader.

DEDICATION

To Mio.

ACKNOWLEDGMENTS

To my wife and my parents.

Thank you for exemplifying healthy sexuality.

You introduced the foundation stone.

PREFACE

Hi, my name is Eddy Kraft. I bought a journal from the bookstore years ago and found it on our family bookshelf, oh, about nine months ago now. Things were a bit different back then, and when I say 'a bit', I'm saying there was a gnarly bit in the horse's mouth that completely changed the direction of my bandwagon...figuratively. Anyway, I ended up naming my journal "Great Gravitations" to be like my favorite novel "Great Expectations" by Charles Dickens, but I'm only a teenager, and he was like a genius writer.

So, a few things happened that triggered me to pull this journal off the shelf, the first being a volleyball game, okay, one of Melanie Westin's volleyball games. It wasn't the game itself that got me journaling, but it was my friend Charles—not Dickens— that I happened to meet at the game. He accused me of having a crush on a volleyball player, i.e. Melanie Westin—it was her fourth turn to serve in the second set because she's pretty good, and I was staring because she's pretty. It was true, and I admitted it. Then after pushing my arm and laughing with me—he's a good school friend—he said that I should journal my thoughts to get them off my chest because sitting like a creepy schoolboy at a volleyball game would only cause me to psychologically implode. Then I asked him why he was there, and he only beat around the bush while the color of his skin turned fuchsia. The little two-timer! Well, that's the first reason for my journaling. The second reason was much greater than the first, and that will take a story to tell, a story that I hope you will find honest and helpful. And yes, it's about Melanie Westin, and yes, it's about sex, and yes, I know it's weird to read my private thoughts about the two, but I figured something out. Not alone, granted. My father, my mother, Mr. Kloomsfield (my health class teacher), and even the famous Solomon (the all-wise one from the Bible that wrote his own book) helped me figure it out, and Melanie Westin helped me prove it was true.

Chapter One

--- *Journal page one hundred and fifty-three of Great Gravitations, my disclaimer.*

I feel kind of like I'm cheating by putting this last entry first, but my mother, when she proofread my story, told me straight up that I should have to 'apologize' for writing such an honestly gruesome thing or should at least 'forewarn' or 'try to explain why' I'd want someone to read the traumatic details of Melanie's experience. Only someone who really loves me would be so candid as my mother, so please accept my apology here and now. Yes, my story is about sex, but I sure didn't write it to awaken anybody's sexual desire and certainly not to teach someone like me to start having pre-marital sex. I wrote it because this same desire, that I mention, awakened inside of me one day not long ago, and I kind of figured it would awaken in nearly everybody sooner or later. Plus, I wanted my classmates to know what actually happened to Melanie and me, and I guess, simply put, how intimacy taught me more about jealousy than it did about pleasure...and how it can seriously mess with your head if you choose to go for it. Scott's in jail by the way, and I think he deserves every bit of what he got from the courts. It's a pitiful five-year sentence if you ask me, and just goes to show that you can't trust what porn depicts on the internet. I'm sure glad my dad caught me and pulled me aside when he had the chance.

--- *The Krafts were all upstairs at the Kraft family's home on 17 Sussex St, before the tempest, before the masque.*

"I have a sandwich waiting for you on the kitchen island, honey," Max Kraft informed as he entered his charmingly decorated master bedroom.

His charming and smartly decorated wife glanced at him as she hastily hoisted a small suitcase onto her side of the bed. "I'm so sorry. And thank you, I know Suzanne will really appreciate me filling in for her speaking engagement while she's sick," Cynthia said, having finished dressing in her normal travel attire slightly behind schedule.

"It's payback time," Max assured, memorizing the fragrance of his wife again.

"I know, but it couldn't be at a worse time with you leaving tomorrow for a month."

"Well, yeah," Max said matter-of-factly. "If you'd prefer, I could hold you hostage and make you miss your flight," Max said and received a momentary glare from his wife. "What are you going to speak on this time?" Max inquired more seriously as he stepped up to properly fold a blouse that his wife had strewn into the suitcase from her third trip to the closet.

"Girl-bonding."

"Girl-bonding's a good one. Hey, I am going to hold you up for a minute," Max insisted, catching his wife on her fifth trip from the closet.

Almost instinctively objecting, Cynthia caught focus of her husband's loving eyes and stopped her hasty commotion to connect with them. "Only for a minute though," Cynthia agreed, playfully kissing her husband.

"Only for a minute, and then I'll go get the car ready," Max said between kisses.

"Ohh, I'm going to miss tonight, and then you're gone for a month to the war zone," Cynthia said, brushing the hair on the back of her husband's head while she scrunched her nose into his cheek.

"There's no war where I'm going; only an hourglass showing me the time I have to wait till I get to touch you again. Minute's up, by the way."

"No," Cynthia whined, childishly. "Time extension."

Max kissed his wife passionately once more and walked out of the room to his son's. He opened Eddy's door and said, "Okay, Ed, it's time to take your mom to the airport."

"Sure, okay," Eddy agreed nervously, forgetting to take his next breath of oxygen as his tan complexion lost its color.

"What are you looking at?" Max asked, noting his son's suspicious behavior and sheltered laptop computer tilted down in his lap.

"Oh, nothing," Eddy excused, moving to comply with his parent's agenda. He stopped to check the status of his dark wavy hair in his dresser mirror like a self-conscious teenager, choosing the normal behavior to fend off the weight of his dad's curiosity.

"Uh-huh, it's a strange phenomenon not being able to see anything with your eyes open," Max said jokingly as he watched his son twitch a comb over his head. "I'll meet you in the car in five. Okay?"

"I'll beat you there," Eddy bet confidently with his get-out-of-jail-free smile.

--- *Journal entry page fifteen, scribbled from the back seat of my dad's car as we drove my mom to the intercontinental airport.*

My dad's a smart guy, and the coolest part about him is that he lets me be me. And part of that allowance is the part where he doesn't make me feel bad about trying new things, even culturally deemed bad things. Like, I was looking at pornography just then, and anyone could see that he knew. But he didn't go freaking out about it, yelling and cursing me to shreds with guilt like my mom probably would have. Some might say that he's a bad parent, but I like him this way. Though, I wonder when he'll find out about how much I like Melanie Westin. "Who is Melanie Westin?" you might ask. She's just the prettiest girl at school.

--- *Jammed in traffic at the mega airport's drop-off point, Max had already placed his wife's suitcase on the curbside.*

"Goodbye, sweetheart," Max said, seeing the energy and remorse mixed together on Cynthia's face. The traffic of bags and people flowed toward the entrance of the airport, and Max let go of his wife so she could join the migration.

Cynthia bent over politely, waved, and blew Eddy a kiss through the open car window. "I'll be home Monday. Be good for your aunt. Okay?"

"Okay, have a good trip, Mom," Eddy expressed from the back seat of the car and watched his mom take inventory of her travel belongings before dashing off into the busy terminal.

"Are you hungry, Ed?" Max asked. "Hey, climb up front why don't you."

"Sure, do I have to cook?"

"I don't know if I trust you playing with natural gas outside of the bathroom," Max answered, spending his attention on the merging traffic. "How about Dobbins Bar and Grill?"

"Sure," Eddy said indifferently to the family-friendly restaurant suggestion.

"I need to talk to you a little about sex."

Immediately connecting the topic to his dad's earlier discovery, Eddy clammed up.

"Unless sex isn't interesting to you."

"No, I'm very interested," Eddy said, acknowledging his silence like a daydreamer returning from a brief ethereal adventure.

"Don't let me make this awkward, but if you would, give me a few minutes to collect my thoughts. I can barely remember my disposition before I started having sex with your mother," Max said and fell quiet as he drove toward the restaurant.

--- *A few quiet and stressful face paws later, inside the comfortable atmosphere of the restaurant, Max broke the silence.*

"Whew, I'm glad you're hungry, cause even if I wasn't, I am now," Max said as he sat down across from his son. A blue-eyed waitress stepped up, took their drink order, and disappeared to the back of the restaurant. Max moved around in his booth, reaching into his front pocket. "I must admit that I'm a little behind the curve on this, and I should have already talked with your mother about it. But here it goes," Max started as he slid a condom across the table. "Do you know what this is?"

"Yeah, a guy had one on in a porn video," Eddy said honestly.

"Good," Max said, debating his next words. "It's called a condom, and it's not a ticket." Max watched Eddy pick it up and twirl it in his fingers. "Put it in your pocket. It's not a ticket to have sex, but it is permission for you to pursue a girl to whatever degree is in that girl's best interest. Do you understand?"

"Yeah."

"What are you guys having?" The waitress asked as she delivered their beverage orders.

"A salad and your soup combo."

"And for me a burger and fries," Eddy added in turn and then flipped closed his menu. His youthful shoulders and tall neck worked together, second-guessing his fallback choice before releasing the menu to the waitress.

"Okay, I'll have those right out," the slim waitress promised and walked away.

"Experience is the only thing between you and having a lifetime of great sex. What my concern is, is this...laziness about sex that's reinforced by pornography and masturbation. Do you know what masturbation is?"

"Yeah," Eddy admitted nervously, tapping an ice cube with his straw.

"You do? Good. Then you know how much fun could lie ahead if you play your cards right," Max said, leaning to his side again. "And pornography only teaches you what girls look like underneath by the way and not a single thing about pleasing a real girl. Only a girl can teach you how to make her orgasm," Max said and looked up from his own glass. "Did porn teach you orgasm and climax too?"

"Yeah."

"I kind of figured society had ditched the school-book method," Max said but read concern on his son's face. "There's nothing wrong...well there's a myriad of things wrong with porn, but your desire to look and your curiosity are not wrong. It's just that porn gets it all wrong. Let me explain."

Eddy balanced his smile like a teeter-totter while analyzing his dad's visible discomfort.

"This isn't easy, and you'd better take notes because you'll be sitting here someday, having had your one shot at getting it right," Max said in response to his son's expression. "If you're interested in sex, you have got to ditch the porn...and the masturbation, for the real thing, for a real girl, while you can, while you still have the drive and energy. Because porn is just flat out easier and quicker and seemingly more adventurous, though it's really not," Max explained and sent his eyes up to a nearby television. "The real adventure comes from pursuing a girl romantically," Max said, itching his scalp at the realness of the word. "And pursuing her in such a way that your moves always jive with her best interest in mind."

Eddy held the straw in his mouth, taking a slow sip occasionally as he listened to his dad.

"I learned a sex secret," Max hinted. "I learned it only years after I had been married to your mom. It took me years to figure this out," Max reiterated, looking at the miniature version of himself to make sure he had his son's attention. "It's the key, I believe, to having a lifetime of great sex, and it only requires one woman. And to put this into perspective, the secret works better when you have sex with the same woman a thousand times. With it, you don't need to lie with a thousand women like the world of porn would have you believe. The porn industry would go out of business if this secret got out," Max said, bouncing his knee up and down underneath the table. "Are you ready for it?"

"Yeah," Eddy said, trying to hide the fact that he was hanging on every word.

"It's the *Song of Songs*," Max said and stared at his son like his point was self-evident. As if he had mispronounced the title, he scrunched his eyes closed, making it look like an explanation was stuck in his subconsciousness. "Okay, before I get to *Song of Songs*, leaping ahead to specifically about sex, great sex, that is, is about, or at least what I've found to be truer than anything else, is only about pleasuring your partner, not yourself. In fact, you don't need to worry at all about pleasuring yourself. That'll happen by design and naturally after you do everything in your power to pleasure her," Max said and took a breath. "It's a simple philosophy, and it's very challenging all at once, and it's crazily bonding, giving rise to terms like: 'she screams for it' and 'can't get enough of it'."

"You say it's challenging. How so?" Eddy interrupted, looking for more information in his dad's rambling.

"It takes time, lots of time...hours of time sometimes. It takes removing the pressure to have sex somehow. You have to cuddle, you have to kiss, you have to romance and sweet talk, and the fascinating part of this romance funnel is...it's work, but it's rewarding work...for you. Here you're doing all you can to serve this girl, and meanwhile you're swimming in euphoria. Do you know what euphoria is?"

"Yes, Dad. School's taught me well."

"One can never assume about school these days," Max said and pushed the air out of the bench cushion with his hand as he repositioned himself. "And that's the entire reason for marriage and companionship. It's to create this fruitful environment. But none of this marriage and partnership stuff works if it's all based on a guy finding his wife or girlfriend sexy enough to ejaculate occasionally. Okay, I said that kind of loudly, sorry."

Eddy laughed to hide his embarrassment and pulled down his right ear with two of his tan knuckles.

"If you get your sense of adventure and your pleasure from porn, there's no need for a girlfriend. Or at least, you'll be conflicted and eventually grow bored of her and start privately looking for a new one, wife, or girlfriend, or whatever," Max said, looking up again at the TV as if he had said his piece and done his part.

Eddy studied his dad's strong face.

"I don't expect you to get all this or have an opinion of any of this yet," Max spoke suddenly, returning his eyes to his son's brown ones. "But I do want you to know that you have permission, not a ticket, but permission to go...engage...a woman...romantically even, so long as you keep her best interest at heart," Max reiterated with a more mature version of Eddy's pleasant expression.

"Thanks. That was a lot easier to swallow than I thought. What do you think Mom would say about all this?" Eddy asked with hesitation, pressing his fingers into his forehead to manage an itch.

"Well, Mom would rather you be celibate until you're thirty-five years old, but she's not blind or dumb to the excitement you're about to experience in romancing a girl."

"So, I'm allowed to date?" Eddy clarified with a hidden energy.

"Umm, yes. Oh my, is that the real time? I completely blanked about your Aunt Kristy. She's probably outside our house right now, ringing the doorbell.

--- Starting in the middle of journal page sixteen as we drove home to our plain-red-brick two-story house.

So, I forgot to mention one thing about Melanie Westin, and it's kind of important. The coolest kid in school, Scott Ardan, has been dating her for a while now, and as rumors have it, they're already having sex regularly. I say 'coolest' as a vanilla stereotype. What I mean is: girls think he's gorgeous and talented, probably because he gets most of the announcer's praise and attention at the school football and baseball games. Nevertheless, I hope Charles doesn't pass along to him word about my crush on his girlfriend, because I'd definitely hate to turn his cocky smile upside down or put his crosshairs on my forehead.

   --- After the tires of the car squeaked into our relatively flat driveway, the car pulsed to a stop behind my aunt's car.

"So, so, sorry. Ed kept complaining how hungry he was, so we had to stop for food," Max said to his sister from the driver's window, bumping his son's arm to play along.

"Oh, I was so hungry," Eddy played flatly.

"Yeah, right. Did you bring me anything?" Kristy asked the pair as she stepped aside so that Max could climb out of the family sedan. Her blond hair, superior height, and fair skin concealed well the fact that she was blood-related to Max, but looks can be deceiving.

"Did I bring you anything?" Max echoed slowly, analyzing why he had been so thoughtless. "A well-fed kid to look after!" Max enthused, feeling the rush of hot air entering the vehicle. "Well, there's half a salad, and a half-eaten hamburger. Pick a box," Max brainstormed apologetically and hoisted the to-go bag in the air.

"Well, it's a good thing I didn't stop at Charley's Pub before I came over," Kristy fumed with sarcasm before relaxing her light and forgiving lips.

After everyone was inside, Eddy hung around the foyer and thumbed through the many empty pages of his journal while Max took Kristy and her small bag up to the guest bedroom. Left alone to eavesdrop on the siblings' conversation, Eddy got a text from his mom, stating that she was on the plane, and he took the unusual initiative to reply, "You're going to do great! Thanks for setting the bar high!" Eddy's phone buzzed again, making him look back down. He laughed at his mom's replying, "Who is this? Give this phone back to my son! — Love."

"So, what's this little rascal been up to lately?" Kristy said as she descended the stairs, her shiny ponytail bouncing lively.

"Sex-ed," came the reply from behind her. "Well, sex-ed starts tomorrow. You're just dying to learn about the female anatomy. Right, Ed?"

"Oh. What adequately inappropriate responses from my brother-child. Are you still playing?" Kristy asked, redirecting the conversation to Eddy while eyeing his guitar in the corner.

"Yeah! Do you want to hear what I've been working on? It's 'Chestnut Broadway' by Sutterfield."

"Why-yes, of course. Entertain me," Kristy said, sinking into one of the two plush couches in the living room.

Max sank right in next to his sister and put his arm comfortably behind her.

"You know your neighbors are going to get the wrong impression with the windows open like this," Kristy teasingly warned.

"Oh, let them gossip about my beautiful sister," Max said before pinching his sister's side.

"Don't you start," Kristy threatened, laughing as seriously as possible before returning a defensive pinch.

Eddy laughed at his father's giddy mannerisms before he started strumming away.

"You've really improved!" Kristy encouraged after the playful fight was subdued by Eddy's creative music and the song had finished.

"Even since last week!" Eddy's dad echoed after clapping proudly. "Well, don't stay up too late. I have to turn in early for an early meeting at 4 a.m. tomorrow morning," Max said, stretching his pant legs as he rose from the couch.

"Ouch."

"I have to catch people awake on the other side of the world before I commit the next twenty-four hours of my existence to traveling there," Max explained as he climbed the stairs. "I'll drop Ed off tomorrow at school on my way to the airport."

"Okay," Kristy replied. "Are you staying up?" Kristy then asked Eddy, interrupting some of his piddling guitar notes.

"For a little bit," Eddy responded with a pick in his mouth.

"Is your homework done?"

"A-yah," Eddy said, stretching a grin across his focused face.

"You up for a movie?"

"Sure," Eddy answered and abandoned his strings with a slap.

--- *My journal, now titled "Great Gravitations", page eighteen.*

Do you know that feeling that happens while dropping your laundry down the laundry chute? Or maybe you don't have a laundry chute like I do. Well, clearing your browser history after having the best sex talk in the history of the world has that same general effect on how you feel. All I can think about as I fall asleep tonight is Melanie Westin and my fourth-hour health class where I'll get to see her.

Chapter Two

Without thinking, Eddy interrupted his morning gab with Kristy and dumped his bowl of wet cereal into the sink. Then running after his dad like there was no tomorrow, he made it to the passenger side of the car with his worn backpack on his shoulder. As the car dipped into the road from the driveway Eddy squinted harshly from the morning sun that was splashing its glory down on the simple neighborhood. Large oaks and humble houses lined the subdivision road, and Eddy noticed a classmate strolling along the sidewalk, hunching forward to support her bookbag.

"How was your meeting this morning?" Eddy asked eagerly, privately hoping to reignite the previous night's dinner topic before his dad left for a month.

"It was clear they needed me to travel back to that god-forsaken place," Max replied, firmly rubbing a spot on his chest while the turn signal of his car winked at a stop sign.

"Well, you like your job, right?" Eddy inquired, relieved at seeing his dad relax after his painful expression.

"I do, but, and this will sound silly, I really don't like being away from your mother for so long," Max admitted as he jetted the car further down the road.

"Dad, if I were to have an opportunity to have sex, how would I make a girl...how would I please her?" Eddy asked while watching his dad scan the road. Eddy's eyebrows wavered on the expression to make, so he licked and stretched his lips to one side instead.

"That's an easy one. Ask for directions, and don't take off your pants before she's pleased."

"I cleared my internet browser last night," Eddy informed, feeling his nerves warm his ears.

"That's a start to the dating process. Hey, and just because you're interested in a girl doesn't mean—"

"I know, Dad."

"Well, it all makes perfect sense if you keep your head focused on what's in her best interest and not on your sex drive," Max said, swiveling his head to check for traffic before turning on the four-lane crossroad. "Just about any girl you run into at school today can make a great companion. Granted, some are closer to being great than others." Max saw that his son was distracted by the approaching school, but he continued, "And I define companionship as how you, Eddy, strive to provide, please, and protect a friend, and they in turn you. Any girl can be great for Eddy, not just the most sexually attractive girl of the moment." Max spoke like his thoughts were on cruise control.

"Any girl," Eddy repeated unintentionally.

"You said it. Now you might not be attracted to that girl, and that's still okay. But remember building a relationship on attraction is the same approach as you'll find with pornography. It's the thousand-women approach, rather that the thousand-intercourses-with-one-woman approach."

"Yeah, yeah. I get that," Eddy laughed uncomfortably, thinking only of Melanie as he eyed the front of the three-story, brown-brick school complex. Students swarmed the front walkways like a morning migration of churchgoers.

"Isn't life so much fun at your age?" Max suggested, grinning at the back of his son's head. "I bet you're thinking: There's no way that short girl in my math class could make me happy," Max critiqued and waited for his son to turn around. "No? Then you're thinking: There's only one girl in this school that's attractive enough to make me happy."

Eddy faced his father after the second guess and silently complimented his father's laser insight.

"It's the *make ME happy* part that will set you up for a pretty quick plateau of blah and unhappiness. Whichever's making you smirk. Just change your thoughts to how can I *make HER happy*. Whether she's short or drop-dead gorgeous. And that might be leaving her alone, or talking to her, or whatever's in her best interest. Just don't send an invitation to your wedding while I'm in Iraq. Okay?"

Eddy chuckled as he lifted his bag up off the floorboard. "Thank you, Dad. I hope you don't mind if I send you questions."

"I'll be checking in on you, Son, and you'd better have some good ones ready!" Max said and tugged his tie back and forth to loosen it while looking at himself in the mirror.

"Bye!"

"Goodbye. Have fun!" Max said and moved out of the drop-off line to exit the parking lot.

Eddy turned around on one heel with a growing grin on his face and walked into the plain lobby of the school. A scattering of students held their pre-morning conversations throughout the lobby, a majority of them standing in small circles and huddled next to the bulletin boards that were on either side of the library doors. The lively lobby stretched in a half-circle around the main office where two secretaries were seated and busily tending to the phones from the morning's slew of sick calls. The tiled floors of the lobby and the four adjoining hallways were a lighter hue of cream than the hundreds of lockers that congested the walls, lockers set with rotary-dial locks that were noisily clicking and clacking away. The welcome of the school was the same as the day before, yet the air in Eddy's lungs was lighter and tasted of promise.

--- Great Gravitations: The top of journal page nineteen, penciled while I leaned against my locker to wait for the warning bell.

There are plenty of students covering the halls, some conversing and most with personal agendas, which gets me thinking about mine. And my dad is so right! Even now as I scope out the school halls, I feel like I'm just checking girls out to grade them. Why does my brain have to be wired so backwards? I'm checking out this girl and that girl, nope, and nope. What about her? Aye...what do I do, Dad? Do I just close my eyes and go for it? Okay.

--- After Eddy clicked his mechanical pencil closed, he shoved the journal-pencil pair into his backpack.

"Hi, Alexis. How tall are you?" Eddy asked a short girl with straight black hair.

"From the looks of it, Ed, about fourteen inches shorter than you. Do you want to measure, or are you good with pointing out my shortcomings for the moment?" Alexis said with sass.

"No, I'm not trying to make fun of you."

"It's a joke, dimwit. Short-comings, cause I'm short. Don't make me feel so bad," Alexis said, bending her brows before turning to walk to class which happened to be the same as Eddy's.

When she noticed Eddy walking beside her, Alexis asked, "Are you following me?"

"No, not at all. We're just on the same course in life for the next one hour and thirty-five seconds."

"Yeesh, do you have to put up with me for that long? I'm sorry," Alexis said, taking the back of her hand and dragging it along the row of lockers.

"Well, I'm not sorry. Hey, what would you rather be doing than math?" Eddy asked, thinking of how ironic it was that his dad had accurately described Alexis and math in the car.

"Judo. Why?" Alexis asked, looking up and over at her classmate.

"Judo! Really! I have no idea what judo is. Will you show me?" Eddy asked with his thumbs under the straps of his backpack.

"Do you want to end up on the floor?" Alexis asked sportively.

"Sure, if it means I'll have a—" Eddy agreed and completely missed his classmate's move to pull him off balance and roll him onto his back. "Oof...a better view. I'd say, you look much taller from down here."

Students nearby stopped to share their curiosity for the unusual happening.

"Here," Alexis offered, beaming at Eddy's roundabout compliment. "Slap my hand away next time."

Eddy grabbed Alexis's hand and asked, "Wow, do you want to go punch out some mathematics now?" He punched the air twice to deliver his pun.

"That's not funny, Ed," Alexis stated and tried to hold back a confession of sarcasm.

"I'll have to try harder then. After you," Eddy ushered.

The lecture started, and the algebraic, dry-erase marks from the teacher on the whiteboard soon lost most of Eddy's interest. Having glanced occasionally at Alexis and being riveted by Alexis's hair color, he leaned over in a lull, as close as he could to

Alexis's ear, and whispered, "I can't decide what color your hair is." Then he straightened himself upright at the prompting of the teacher.

"Ed, do you have something to share with the class?"

"Yes," Eddy said, panicking as he searched his thoughts for what would fix the moment. The answer appeared on the board. "Y is not I over U is not grammatically correct, sir."

The class took a moment and looked at the board. Some giggled at the equation the teacher had legitimately written.

"I just wanted to share some humor I saw, sir," Eddy said, nearly breaking a sweat.

"And you just might have made my day, Ed. Thank you, shall we continue?"

"Now that was funny," Alexis whispered, leaning her short torso as far over the aisle as Eddy had when the teacher had turned his back.

Eddy bubbled like a glowing lava lamp and wrote a message on his notepad that read, "WHAT COLOR IS YOUR HAIR?" Then slowly, he lifted it up for Alexis to read without shifting his gaze from the whiteboard.

"Dark brown. Stop distracting me," Alexis wrote in reply across her own blank page.

"Okay," Eddy wrote boldly on a new page and caught Alexis grinning from a proud glance he took at her profile.

--- Two class periods later, Eddy paid his toll to the tired-looking lunch lady who regularly collected his lunch money.

"Well, who would've thunk?" Eddy said, walking up to Alexis, who had just arranged herself at a long lunch table by herself. "Are you sitting with anybody?"

"No, go ahead take it," Alexis invited courteously and reached over to relocate her bookbag.

"Gladly," Eddy replied with a loud thumping heart as he picked up Alexis's food tray with his free hand.

"Hey!" She complained. "I meant the seat!"

"Follow me, judo master," Eddy invited, already having taken two steps toward his destination.

Containing her frustration over her new friend, she picked up her bag and caught up to Eddy.

"How are you guys doing today?" Eddy asked as he set the two trays in front of two open seats at a busy table.

"Those seats are taken."

"Oh, sorry, I should have asked," Eddy apologized without continuing his attempt to sit. Then lifting the trays up overhead, he turned around to the busy table behind him and asked if the two spots were open. After getting somewhat of a yes, he set the trays down and had Alexis sit down before he slid into his spot.

"Hey, Alexis," someone greeted from across the table.

"Hey, Sarah," Alexis replied and started eating her food.

"Alexis, do you know Cassidy?" Sarah asked, her sweet voice as inviting as an early morning birdsong.

"No. It's nice to meet you, Cassidy," Alexis replied, extending her hand firmly to the girly-girl that had curled her naturally straight hair to be as curly as her seatmate's.

"Careful shaking her hand. She's a judo master," Eddy informed.

"Stop it!" Alexis commanded, playfully hitting Eddy's chest.

"What? That's not what you told me about your hands earlier. I asked her to show me a judo move earlier, and before I could blink, she had me on my back, looking up at her dark brown hair."

"Are you guys together?" Cassidy asked, suspecting such.

"You mean like sitting together?" Eddy asked, almost blushing as he glanced around at the different observant faces.

"No, like are you guys dating?" Cassidy clarified, standing her ground for an answer.

"Umm, I don't believe we've defined our classmate-ship with that term yet. Have we?" Eddy asked, twisting his shoulder around to face Alexis in their confined space.

Alexis answered, "You're not my type."

"I'm not her type," Eddy comically relayed, wrapping his arm slowly around Alexis's back to Sarah and Cassidy's entertainment.

"Ugh."

"And don't get any ideas," Alexis said and snorted after she elbowed Eddy's gut.

"No. I have no ideas, friend Alexis."

"Liar."

"I only lie half the time," Eddy said, picking up his food again.

"Seriously, you guys are flirting," Sarah equally accused, contagiously giggling over the interchange.

"No, seriously, Sarah, you have captivating eyes. What color are they?" Eddy asked.

"Hazel…and thank you."

"What's your fascination with colors today, Edward?"

"Did you know her eyes were hazel?" Eddy defended against Alexis's aggravated accusation.

"No," Alexis admitted. "But does it matter?"

"It for certain does matter! Like, like, come on, what are you going to say to the driver's license people if you don't know your eye color?" Eddy rationalized spontaneously.

"I didn't know your full name was Edward," Sarah noted.

"No, it's not actually. I'm named after a water phenomenon. It's just Eddy, and thank you, Sarah, for asking. See, Alexis? Hey, Alexis," Eddy said, catching Alexis's elbow as she slid out of the seat.

Alexis recoiled back to Eddy and floated her lips out of view of the interested classmates that sat across the table. "Hey, Ed, I'd just like to eat alone if that's okay," Alexis politely whispered.

"Sure, sure, I'll catch up with you later. Don't study too hard," Eddy said, leaning back from the line of students. He saw Alexis look over her shoulder as she continued her retreat.

"Did I offend her?" Sarah asked.

"No," Eddy said, scrunching his dark eyebrows and shaking his head to add conviction to his answer.

"So, you guys really aren't dating then?" Sarah asked, smiling as she observed Eddy's darker locks of hair start to bounce with his answering head shake.

"No, and really no. She sits next to me in math, and we seemed to hit it off this morning, but," Eddy said, shrugging to finish his thought.

"So, you're interested in dating her then," Cassidy pushed, interpreting Eddy's open-ended remark.

"Well, yeah. Who wouldn't be interested in dating her?"

"You'd have to bend halfway over to kiss her," an eavesdropper commented.

"Ooh okay," Eddy replied as if the comment were childish. "And she would have to bend over if I was kneeling, but why are we jumping downstream?" Eddy asked and put some food in his mouth.

"Does your mom even allow you to date?" Cassidy asked. "Your mom's like a Christian speaker, right?"

"She is, and she has a new book out called *Why Isn't Dating Still a Thing* by Cynthia Kraft."

"Really?" Cassidy asked perplexed.

"Not really, but that would make a compelling title. Don't you think? Actually, my dad gave me permission to date, kind of behind my mother's back."

"My parents wouldn't even think about letting me date," Cassidy admitted, letting out a bit of envy in her voice.

"And do you think your parents have your best interest in mind?" Eddy prompted Cassidy between bites.

"So, if your dad gave you permission to date, what does that mean about having sex?" Sarah asked before recognizing her question would garner great attention.

"That is a very pointed question, Sarah. He didn't forbid it, and he definitely gave me a talking to about it," Eddy said, putting more food in his mouth in an attempt to make the topic disappear.

"Don't dodge the question. Does permission to date give you permission to have sex?" a student down the table reiterated.

"A pointed question made pointier, but I have an answer for you, Rod. I don't think you can get permission from your parents to have sex, that can only be given from the person you're dating. And hopefully there's more reasons for dating that person than just having sex."

"So, would you have sex with a girl who gave you permission?" someone else asked.

"Who put a dartboard on my forehead? Yeah, I'd want to if it was in her best interest," Eddy replied, his boldness waning.

The warning bell interrupted the tribunal, and Eddy looked around at the smiling faces that were frequently glancing at him as he finished his lunch in double time.

Chapter Three

The most run down, and hence least utilized, bathrooms in the school were outside the cafeteria. These were at the bottom of the double-wide flight of stairs that zigzagged up to the main floor and into the school's lobby. Eddy walked out of the cafeteria, passed the bathrooms, and climbed the steps, looking for Alexis, but she was nowhere to be seen.

Charles, a scrawny yet faithful classmate that could be characterized by the stiffness of his dress clothes, saw Eddy and met up with him.

"Hey, we missed you at lunch today," Charles said and assumed Eddy's posture with his hands clutching his backpack straps.

"Yeah, I was just making some new friends."

"We're still friends, right?" Charles asked.

"Of course. You should float around with me on Monday."

"It's not really my thing to float, but the guys were pointing you out. Be sure to float back our way sometimes," Charles admonished. With his concern delivered, he waved as he reversed his direction and stiffly marched back down the steps toward the English hallway that was isolated in the back wing of the school.

Eddy stopped and waved in reply, chuckling to himself at the possessiveness of Charles' behavior. Then for a moment, he wanted to disappear as Melanie Westin approached and accidentally bumped his shoulder in passing. A short apology and a generic smile that fit contritely between her prior string of words appeared like a shooting star in his piece of the sky, and just as briefly too, but the star's astronomical trajectory curled away from him like it had been affected by the ever so constant string and pull of the planet. Not missing a beat on her conversational re-entry, Melanie walked away aside her giggly and girly friend toward the central stairwell. Health class was next.

"Somebody pinch me," Eddy instructed as he caught himself staring.

"Dude, I hear you're having sex now. Welcome to the club!" Scott Ardan said, enthusiastically grabbing both of Eddy's shoulders and shaking them as he stepped by to pursue Melanie.

"Club? Wow! Do I get a pin for being in the club?" Eddy asked randomly, moving half the speed of Scott toward the doublewide flight of stairs.

"Pin? No, dude. You get a score card!" Scott said, shunning Eddy as he draped his arm over his girlfriend to pull her out of her orbital conversation.

Eddy walked, ebbing further behind the infatuation of his life, and likewise, when he reached the top of the stairwell, he veered to the left, stepped by Scott and Melanie's intimate hallway conversation, and entered Steven Kloomsfield's classroom.

"Come in; sit anywhere you like. I know the chairs are rearranged. We're starting a new topic today, and we'll be changing seats shortly. So, don't get too comfortable, and there's no need to get out your books," Steven orated a few times over as students filtered into the classroom with curious expressions.

"So, I guess we get to sit with the sex therapist," Sarah said to Cassidy as they sat down next to Eddy.

"Oh my, really? I hope you're making that up. I only know what someone else has told me about sex which is not a qualification for being a sex therapist. And I just said sex more times in one sentence than I have all year," Eddy fretted as his hands curled up around his head.

"You kind of put yourself in the spotlight at lunch," Sarah added, laughing at Eddy's overreaction.

"Me? Spotlight? Who was accusing me of dating Alexis?" Eddy criticized falsely. "I'm just joking, Sarah," Eddy assured, lowering his hands and leaning forward in Sarah's direction to convince her.

"Watch out for this guy! He's got your panties on his mind," Scott said proudly from over Eddy's head. Scott usually waited for the tardy bell before he stepped into the classroom, and the tardy bell in fact was calling him to his seat as he lofted his big-talking words over the table.

Sarah and Cassidy looked unappreciative as Scott maneuvered to a spot next to Melanie in the back of the room.

"Well that makes this totally awkward," Eddy said and stood up slowly with an overly ghostly face as if he was going to change seats to remedy the vulgar remark.

Sarah laughed.

"Sit down, Ed," Steven Kloomsfield instructed. "You don't need to prove that you're taller than me."

Eddy sat down, glad to have the shortest guy teacher in the school shew him away from the spotlight.

"As I've said, we will be switching seats after our initial talk about family planning, and don't everybody cheer at once. We will be discussing sex in every way possible, to include safety, pregnancy, contraception, which is a part of safety, personal responsibility, child-rearing, and the list goes on," Steven Kloomsfield said, listing everything in an overly forlorn voice. Then dropping his attention to his role-call list, he switched to a real tone and continued, "Those are the parts that we have to cover according to—"

"Mr. Kloomsfield, if you need us to, we can sexually educate the class with a demonstration," Scott interjected, before getting punched in the arm by Melanie.

"Please don't, Scott. I think you underestimate the intellects of your classmates."

"Well, then can Melly and I take the test now and boogie, 'cause we already know about condoms and stuff."

Steven Kloomsfield eschewed answering and continued, "What I'm more interested in, and what I hope you're more interested in, are the opinions out there surrounding the topic of sex. What do I mean? There are different theories on human sexuality just like there are different political parties or different cultures. Can anybody name a couple popular ones?" Steven asked, and trustingly looked for a student to answer.

"Heterosexuality and homosexuality are two parts of the topic," a student finally answered.

"That's 100% correct, but I'd like to focus on ideological positions rather than gender issues," Steven said and cast his eyes about for a different answer. "Well, it's estimated that nearly 75% of you here today have gotten your opinions about human sexuality from each other or from the media. Raise your hand if you'd say that's true," Steven said and looked around at a proportionally correct number of hands. "Then, 10% of you have been educated by your parents and another 15% have no influencing opinion whatsoever," Steven continued while setting his clipboard down and folding his hands together out in front of him. After assessing his audience, he turned around and wrote the statistics on the whiteboard. "My hope is that the 10% of you that have been blessed enough to have a parent's sexual education will be willing to share it for the benefit of the rest of the class. Then in return, I hope the 75% of your peers that have gleaned their information from private sources will be willing to share their privileged information," Steven said, looking to both sides of the classroom. Still sensing the tension, he continued, "To put everyone at ease, nothing expressed here during these first three days of class will be quizzed or examined in any way." Steven looked around for a consensus of attention. "Be honest now; who wants to know what parents are saying? I promise I won't call on you to speak if you raise your hand...this time anyway."

Eddy raised his hand. Then unpretentiously, Cassidy and a few others followed.

"Okay, what about the flip side? Who wants to know what the word on the street is?"

More hands went up slowly till Steven refused to wait any longer.

"Let's start with the ten percent of you that have heard from your parents. Will anybody who has heard from a parent be willing to answer the question, 'When and with whom should you have sex with?'"

"My parents told me that sex is sacred and should only be had between a man and a woman after marriage," Cassidy reported, subconsciously pulling at and straightening the curls of her sandy-blond hair.

"That's a very common and good answer. Anyone else?"

"To be responsible, and not get a girl pregnant," someone else said.

"We'll talk a lot about that. Good answer."

"Eddy's parents just gave him permission to start having sex," Scott interjected.

"Oh, are you his spokesman? I had no idea," Steven Kloomsfield fired back sarcastically enough to make the class laugh.

"They didn't give me like a ticket to start having sex, per say," Eddy defended, bending his body nervously to the side. "But my dad did sit me down and pointed out the stark differences between pornography and companionship. I don't know how much detail you want," Eddy said, drumming the table with all of his fingers twice.

"The floor is yours. Speak for the benefit of the ninety percent."

"My dad told me essentially that whatever is on the foundation of a relationship determines how long it will last. If it's like pornography, based solely on sexual attraction, it'll last until someone else is more attractive, or in other words not for very long. But, if it's based on companionship, where sex is the best time of your relationship, you're gonna be in for a good time," Eddy said, and flicked his eyes between the table and the teacher. "He didn't use all of those words, but that was his main point, I think," Eddy said and formulated his next thought when he saw everyone seemed to be awaiting a further explanation. "Then he told me about how girls respond differently to sex than boys do. Again, he described how pornography had romance backwards, where girls need more time, sometimes hours of more time, cuddling, kissing, and so on before they're ready...before they're satisfied. Is this the information you're looking for?" Eddy asked, feeling the giddiness rising in the room like carbonation in an open soda bottle.

"So, how would your dad answer the question, 'When and with whom should you have sex with?'" Steven prompted from his comfortable posture on his stool.

"Oh, that's easy, have sex with someone when it's in their best interest, and he emphasized 'their best interest' a bunch," Eddy answered, and he leaned back in his chair, feeling the tug between confidence and embarrassment color his cheeks.

"Thank you, those were all good answers. How about the word on the street, Scott?" Steven asked intentionally for sake of his prior interruptions.

"Have sex with whomever. We're not married. She's on birth control. We just do it whenever we feel like it. If we wanted to have sex with other people, we wouldn't stop each other," Scott spoke decidedly.

"It's nice that you included me in your answer, Scott," Melanie interjected almost as sarcastically as the teacher had earlier.

"Well, do you agree with Scott? Open sex with whomever and whenever you feel like it?" Steven pressed, crossing his arms as he rested on his stool.

"Well, yeah it has to feel right. But I think I agree more with what Eddy was saying, that girls need more time, and if you find someone who gives you the attention you need, that's a good reason to stick with that person. If they stop, then you move on and find someone else," Melanie said and nervously started rocking one of her legs back and forth.

"Both are good answers. So, if I may, I'd like to categorize these ideologies for you, just to facilitate our discussion. There's abstinence, that's my term, meaning sex is only for marriage. There's open sex, again my term, meaning sex with anyone as you please. And there's some sort of middle ground, meaning sex based on mutual terms. On Monday, I want those who are interested in discussing abstinence sitting here, middle ground here, and open sex sitting there, and mind you there's no permanent seating assignments for the next few days," Steven said, pointing distinctly at and then between each table to loosely emphasize his point. "We are going to have a discussion, to figure out the pros and cons of each position on Monday and have a cross-examination of those positions on Tuesday. These are not discussions to prove any one side is right or wrong but for you to go home and consider the reasons why you hold the views you do. Then, we'll get to the required learning," Steven explained and shifted his attention to the door to receive the note from the hallway runner.

The runner handed the note and glanced briefly at Eddy before walking out.

"Ed, you're needed in the office for an early dismissal. Go ahead and take your things."

Still bubbling with latent energy from his honest interview with the teacher, Eddy reddened more as he picked up his bag.

"Looks like Slick Dick's changing tables already," Scott commented as everyone watched Eddy leave the room.

Eddy ignored Scott's vie for laughs and idled behind the hall runner. The reasoning for his dismissal was of idle importance too because his mind was fully preoccupied with the fact that Melanie had said his name and had said that she at least partly agreed with him about his dad's sex secret. "Thank you, Dad! I can't wait to tell you about this one!" Eddy said to his nearly empty locker as he emptied and restocked his bookbag.

His locker was about a bowling-alley stretch from the front lobby and the main office, and as he walked up to the window, he saw Kristy sitting quietly inside. Her hair always fell just right, and today was no different. When Eddy cracked open the door, Kristy's eyes latched onto him, and she rose to her feet in a confusing manner as if Eddy were the doctor arriving to deliver his prognosis.

"Hi, Kristy, what's up?" Eddy greeted, looking for a 'last minute work emergency' or 'forgotten doctor's appointment' to proceed from her mouth.

Kristy forced a heroic look. "Eddy."

Ed looked at the secretary seated behind her desk as she blew her nose and tried to hide a sob. Her eyes and nose were red like she was tearing up with joy and sick with a runny nose all at once.

The principal and the counselor appeared like two bank managers in their office doorways.

"Eddy," Kristy repeated, reaching for his hand.

"Miss Kristy, Eddy, let's talk in here," the principal invited, and he motioned for the two Kraft's to take a seat in the counselor's office.

Kristy started to try to hold back sobs as the principal closed the door to the office and pulled up the extra chair from the corner of the room.

"What happened?" Eddy asked, starting to feel Kristy's emotion seep under his skin.

"I'm sorry, Eddy," Kristy said, shunning Eddy's eyes as he looked around the room for his answer. "I'm sorry; I'm going to be sick," Kristy said to the principal and rose promptly to her feet to flee the office.

"Does she need to go to the doctor? Cause I can walk home if that's the case," Eddy reasoned, trying to line up the confusing observations.

"Eddy, your dad...," the counselor said and hid his stiff chin with a few of his fingers. "The authorities called your house today around lunch time and reported to your aunt that your dad had collapsed at the airport due to what they believe was a heart attack. And he didn't make it to the hospital. He passed away before he got to the hospital. I called the hospital a few minutes ago. And they kindly confirmed everything."

Eddy sat for a moment of reflection. "He's on an airplane headed to a settlement in Iraq."

The counselor took a deep breath, and the principal moved over to the chair Kristy had vacated.

Eddy shrewdly retrieved his mobile phone and poked aggressively at it. Then after a few heart-pounding inner quakes, he lifted the phone to his ear. "Dad, call me as soon as you get this," he spoke after his dad's voicemail prompt, and he looked up to see the male counselor dabbing his eyes. He then started typing out the same message that would be sent to his dad directly on the airplane, assuming his dad had an internet connection.

The principal laid his hand on Eddy's shoulder.

"No!" Eddy said, jerking his shoulder away and standing to his feet. He left the office with the phone to his ear again. "Sergeant Brock, this is Eddy Kraft, Max's son. He's supposed to be traveling to Iraq today."

"That's right. He should be airborne now. Would you like me to relay a message to him when he lands?" the liaison officer offered in his usual, helpful manner.

"No," Eddy said, supporting himself with the wall outside the office.

"Is everything okay?" the familiar officer asked, detecting Eddy's distress.

"They said he didn't make it."

"Well, I can certainly check with the airline, and if he didn't, we can just put him on a flight tomorrow. That'd just mean you'd get to spend another night with him, my man. I'll check and call you back, Eddy," the officer said optimistically. "Eddy? I'll call you back, okay?"

"They said he didn't make it to the hospital," Eddy replied, wiping his face with his shirt sleeve.

"Oh," Sergeant Brock exhaled, and listened as the implications started swirling around the silence. "Wow. I didn't see that one coming. I'm sorry, Eddy," he said, hoping for the right words to come. "I guess...I guess that makes you the man of the house now. Are you at school? Is someone around you, Eddy?"

"Yeah," Eddy said, closing his eyes to hide himself from the lights of the office.

"Well, don't keep this one inside. Don't keep this one inside, my friend. It's perfectly okay to ask to talk to a counselor...even if you don't need to talk," Sergeant Brock said and listened for some sort of feedback.

"They know," Eddy admitted. "Thank you."

"You're welcome, Eddy. I'll miss him."

"Me too," Eddy said and hung up the phone.

Kristy walked up to Eddy and put both her arms around him before he could sink to the floor.

"Is it true?" Eddy asked, unable to control the timbre of his voice as his chin rested on his aunt's petite shoulder.

--- Seven hundred and forty-three miles away at the front of the audience-filled room in the House Royal Hotel and Conference Center.

"Great job, Cynthia!" the stage coordinator complimented as Cynthia cleared the two-foot-high stage. Cynthia accepted her compliment while smoothing her flowery dress. Her tapered, auburn, bob haircut looked unchanged, but she self-consciously checked it again in the stage mirror anyway. The applause thinned out from behind Cynthia as she stepped deeper into the backroom and grabbed her small towel to dab her forehead and armpits. The stage coordinator ran back and forth in the room like a bumble bee debating two luscious flowers. "Hey, I hope you don't mind, I put it on silent mode. It's been ringing off the hook," the stage coordinator rushed to say in passing, handing

Cynthia her phone before moving off to introduce the next speaker on the other chatter-filled side of the wall.

"Thank you," Cynthia warmly said, trying to release her speech jitters. Her penciled eyebrows raised when she saw nine missed calls, five voices mails, and three text messages. "I didn't speak that much over, did I?" Cynthia joked to herself.

She raised the phone above her noticeable cheekbone and listened to the first voicemail.

A gruff voice spoke, "Hi, my name is Sargeant Griffey. I'm with the county police, and I need to inform you of the status of a Maxwell Kraft. This is the emergency contact number listed on his identification. He has collapsed here at the airport due to symptoms we believe are from a heart attack. He is currently being transported to Lawton Hospital via ambulance. There is no need to return this call, please forward your questions to the hospital...."

Cynthia was worried as she scrambled for a pen to write down the phone number. Unable to find one before the message ended. She sat down ready to copy the next number. "Heavenly Father, please keep his heart going," she vocalized.

"Hi, my name is Karen Fawcett at Lawton Hospital," the somber voice introduced. "I'm calling for a Cynthia Kraft with urgent information regarding her husband, Maxwell Kraft."

Cynthia scribbled down the phone number to the hospital. "Merciful Father, put Max in good hands."

"Cynthia, you have to call me when you get this," Kristy frantically spoke clearly in distress.

"God? Please?"

"Hi, Mrs. Kraft, this is Shaun Clapton from High Gate, I've received word from Kristy Kraft, who we have here on file as an authorized guardian for your son, Eddy. I don't know if you're aware of your husband's status, please accept my deepest condolences. I wanted to touch base with you before I pull Eddy out of class to tell him. Kristy is here, and I've called the hospital to confirm...."

Cynthia was biting her lip to keep it from shivering. A few attendees glanced at her, but they walked by to give her privacy.

After skimming over the similarly urgent and confirming text messages from Kristy, her phone buzzed. She tapped the new message. "I'm home now. When are you coming back? — Eddy."

--- At the same moment, Eddy sought comfort from the confines of his shaggy bedroom carpet.

Eddy lay on his bedroom floor alone for an hour, listening to Kristy move around the house. After he heard Kristy having a phone conversation with his mother through the floorboards, he pushed himself upright. Then after staring at a picture set on his desk of his father and him, he wiped away new tears and walked downstairs to make himself a sandwich.

"Are you okay?" Kristy asked.

"I'm fine. I'm going to go eat this in my room," Eddy said, attempting to replace his sadness with indifference. Eddy's brown eyes were lost until they at last found and fixated on his cold knuckles that gripped the staircase banister.

"Okay," Kristy said with uncertainty from her position on the couch, the position where she had sat next to her brother for the last time.

Eddy went up and took a bite of his bland sandwich before flopping down amidst his scattered bed covers. After an hour of staring at the painted popcorn ceiling, he fell asleep.

--- Great Expectations: Journal page twenty, with a mindless pencil mark on the top left of the page where I would have recorded the date.

I woke up at 10:30 p.m. hungry. I finished eating my sandwich. Blah. My phone had thirteen messages. At least it feels good to not be the only one that's sad. Then a porn titled e-mail was in my inbox. I went to click on it, but I couldn't bring myself to do it, not with my dad hovering somewhere over my head. I guess that's a good thing. I'm glad it's the weekend. What I want now, more than anything, is to remember exactly what my dad had said over dinner, so I can write it down for Monday's class. All I can remember, though, is him saying, "It's in the *Song of Songs*," which I've read like four times over since yesterday, and it's not jogging my memory. Oh, I know he said something about it taking girls longer to have an orgasm and, then in the car, to leave my pants on. Who cares if the class chuckled. I don't care if they chuckle again. It's my dad. I remember him saying that, and then saying that all I need to worry about is pleasing the girl, but I know he said something else, a few things, a few really important things after that, and it's bothering me like one of my vocabulary words this week, egregiously!

Chapter Four

Cynthia eagerly gathered her things to get off the aircraft, and as she had her head buried under her seat, an announcement came over the passenger address system. "We are looking for a Cynthia Kraft. Cynthia Kraft, would you please see the gate agent at the top of the jet bridge. Cynthia Kraft, please see the gate agent at the top of the jet bridge."

"What now?" Cynthia protested to herself.

Cynthia followed the line of passengers off the airplane and approached the counter.

"Hi, I'm Cynthia Kraft," she said to one of the attendants.

"Here she is," the attendant relayed to a woman dressed in a suit.

"Mrs. Kraft, hi. I'm Michelle Thompson, the station manager here for the airline. We got word of your husband's situation and wanted to express our deepest condolences. This is for you," Michelle said somberly and extended a card.

Cynthia accepted the gift and nervously said, "Thank you, I just really want to get home."

"Well, please, if I may offer you our services to compliment any travel arrangements you've made. I do know from the information we've collected that your husband's car is in one of our affiliate parking lots, and I can take you there right from the jet bridge, or I can shuttle you to the baggage and arrivals area if you have other arrangements," Michelle courteously offered.

"My husband's car would be convenient."

"Certainly, one second. Where would you like your checked bag delivered?" Michelle asked as she took over the computer station from the working gate agent.

"Home, please."

"And home is 17 Sussex St.?" Michelle asked, referencing Cynthia's booking information from behind the computer station.

"Yes, ma'am," Cynthia acknowledged, looking around the boarding area at the congregated passengers.

"Done. Just follow me," Michelle said and oddly led Cynthia back into the jet bridge.

--- *In less than an hour later, having traveled from jet-bridge to front door, Cynthia pushed herself with her carryon into her empty foyer.*

"Hey, Eddy!? Kristy?" Cynthia called as she entered.

"Hey, Cynthia!" Kristy said, shuffling her light feet into the foyer like she was ready to fight the wind back out of the house. "I'm so sorry," Kristy offered with an affectionate embrace. "It's okay, it's okay," Kristy said as she felt the resoluteness of her sister-in-law burst open. As if Cynthia's knees had just learned the news, they weakened, and Kristy clung to her sister-in-law, refusing to let her sink down in her distress.

For a long while, Cynthia cried and cried, muffled on Kristy's patient yet eroding shoulder. And when her harsh waves of realization had lessened and the first of her dense oceans of agony had been shed, with apologies for her sobbing so stubbornly refuted, the pair moved further into the house.

"Someone just dropped off your bag a few minutes ago. I was kind of surprised," Kristy commented as she walked by Cynthia's luggage. "I thought they only did that kind of thing when your bag was lost."

Cynthia had still only in part pulled herself together, and it took her a few glances between the rooms to make sense of Kristy's observation. "They went above and beyond, taking me to Max's car in a limo. They even had a signed card from the airline employees."

"Are you hungry?" Kristy asked without hearing Cynthia's response for sake of her own loud thoughts.

"Almost," Cynthia said, detecting a rumbling of footsteps flying down the stairs.

"When was the last time you've eaten?" Kristy inquired.

"I, I haven't."

"Mom, welcome home," Eddy said and beelined straight to hug his mom. Releasing her after a rushed moment, he walked to the refrigerator.

"Are you okay, Ed?" Cynthia asked.

"Yeah, but I need to get back to studying," Eddy said indifferently, grabbing a yogurt followed by a spoon. While peeling back the yogurt's lid, he scuffled along the reflective hardwood floor back to the staircase and returned to his mountain cave.

"Well, you had best know, Cynthia, that I'm not going anywhere until life settles down," Kristy promised when Cynthia's steady eyes, like a periscope, returned from trying to decode her son's perplexing dash to his room. Then ushering the tired traveler to one of the tall seats in the family kitchen, Kristy went on to silently present the traveler her simple, yet thoughtfully prepared, dinner.

--- *On the following Monday morning, the chaotic school lobby rustled with myriads of feet and voices.*

"Hey, man, I'm sorry to hear about your dad," Charles offered, finding Eddy as he rounded the corner of his locker's hallway. Charles's loose poof of curly hair and thick glasses had not changed in popularity over the weekend.

"Thanks," Eddy simply responded.

"If you need a shoulder to cry on, let me know," Charles said like an unrelating adolescent.

"I'll be okay, but thank you," Eddy said, forcing happiness for a moment, and he continued walking down the front hallway toward his locker.

"Hey, I heard about your dad passing away, Ed," Cassidy said, approaching Eddy as he dialed in his lock combination. "I've been thinking about you all this weekend and wanted to express my condolences."

"Thank you, Cassidy," Eddy replied, not knowing whether to look at his personal compartment or at Cassidy's face.

Seeing Eddy indecisively glance at her, Cassidy respectfully moved on toward her class.

"Mr. Kraft, I'm glad I caught you. If you need any time over the next few weeks, please just let your teachers know and come hide in any of our offices, okay?" the principal offered, having intentionally waited for him at the door of his first classroom.

"Thanks."

"I personally let your teachers know over the weekend, and each one expressed their condolences, just so you're aware."

"Thank you," Eddy said, allowing the principal to place his firm hand on his shoulder.

Eddy walked quietly into his math class and sat down next to Alexis. "Hey, Alexis, may I apologize for yesterday?"

"What'd you do? Egg my house or something?"

"I mean on Friday at lunch time," Eddy corrected, holding his gaze long enough to make her try to look away twice.

"Don't you dare ask me what color my eyes are!"

"No," Eddy laughed after he had lost hold of his thought. "I felt like I made you uncomfortable, and I wanted to apologize."

"Apology accepted. I had fun. You were funny," Alexis said, licking her fingers from the bag of potato chips she had finished eating.

"Hey, Eddy, I'm sorry about your dad," a student from his music class said in passing.

"What happened to your dad?" Alexis said brashly out of curiosity.

"He died of a heart attack this past Friday," Eddy explained.

"Oh," Alexis said rigidly, suspending the crumpling of her chip bag. "Well, I feel dumb and out of the loop."

"Don't feel bad. I'm glad word is spreading," Eddy said, happy for a breath of honesty.

--- *Great Gravitations: Journal page twenty-seven, written after school in the kitchen with a jellyroll yet to be eaten beside me.*

I'm usually pretty good about blocking out distractions so that I can pay attention, but today, the mixture of my dad, the apologies, and the looming sex-ed presentation all made my first three classes feel like a blur. Walking through the lunch line, I noticed that I was just pathetically smiling at people's attempted condolences. Among the many groups, Alexis was conveniently sitting alone again.

--- *Earlier, with lunch tray in hand, Eddy approached Alexis.*

"May I join you?"

"If you don't steal my tray, sure," Alexis said, allowing her eyes a reprieve to look up from her food.

Eddy sat down two spaces away from Alexis and lowered his bag to the floor.

"Really?" Alexis objected and picked up her bag and slid over two spaces to where she was touching Eddy's shoulder with hers. "You could have sat there without asking."

Eddy's cheeks rose long enough to make his response authentic, and then he plunged to eating in silence. This silence was graciously respected below the crowd of voices that laughed unawares about the room. When Eddy had discovered his last shovel of food, he moved to pull out his list of sex-ed notes. "Thank you, by the way, for not talking my ear off," Eddy remarked, finally looking over and perceiving his muteness.

"Oh, do I come across as a big mouth to you?" Alexis investigated, tilting her head forward to get a look at Eddy's face.

"No, small mouth, quick mouth, or pretty mouth would better describe you," Eddy said, looking back down at his notes.

"There you go flirting again," Alexis accused.

"Which part was flirting?" Eddy asked passively and looked up to gauge whether Alexis was offended or pleased.

"This is the first day this year that I wore lipstick and any type of makeup, so for you to call me pretty means you were looking."

"It looks good."

"Thank you," Alexis said. "Now go talk some sex into Steven Kloomsfield's sex-ed class."

"What?"

"Did I say sex or sense?" Alexis reviewed, tensing her eyebrows as she picked up her bag. "It's a pun, dufus, and don't get any ideas."

"Pun taken," Eddy said as he watched Alexis walk away before turning back to his presentation notes. As he finished skimming the page, Charles slapped him on the arm and said, "See you in fifth period."

The touch made Eddy realize the time, and he responsively slammed his book closed on his notes and vacated the cafeteria.

--- *After beating the strike of the school bell to his fourth period, Eddy paid attention from his seat at the center table in his Family Planning class.*

"Okay, here's how it's going to go down. You'll present from up here, and I want to get through as many presenters as possible. So, we will go from group to group until we run out of time. Try to limit your presentation to no more than five minutes," Steven Kloomsfield said, dragging a lectern over to the center of the whiteboard. "Obviously presenting is optional. After someone is finished presenting, no questions please, but I would like you to write your own pros up on the board while the next presenter gets ready," Steven Kloomsfield instructed and wrote large headers on three parts of the board that corresponded to each table. The room was silent as he took a straight edge and made a perfectly flat line under each title. "So, now for the part where I scratch my head. Who wants to present their views on this ever-present issue?" Steven asked, letting his eyes inform the class that he had finished his instructing.

Eddy raised his hand and looked around.

"Ed. I want to hear what Ed has to say. And this is not who wants to present first, but who all wants to present. Anyone else? Because if not, you'll get to listen to me make a textbook case for each of the other two silent tables, and that should sound about as much fun as I am tall," Steven forewarned, still surveying the classroom. "Cassidy, thank you," Steven said, and wrote Cassidy's name under Eddy's. "Anyone from the open sex group? Anybody else? Again, this is all for you," Steven reiterated and waited as long as he could bear. "Well, it'll be a short day then. Eddy, you're up!" Steven summoned and retreated to his desk in the corner where his standard issue filing cabinet, lackluster bookshelf, and antiquated computer were castled together.

Eddy took the lectern, having prepared so intensely over the weekend because of his dad. Then seeing that almost every student looked uncomfortable, he grinned and arranged his notes out in front of him. "Thank you, Mr. Kloomsfield, for having us do this," Eddy opened, looking directly at the teacher. "Initially when I set out preparing, I wanted to present every word my dad had told me over dinner last week, and I got to writing down all that I could remember. However, the harder I focused on trying to remember his words the fuzzier they got in my memory, and there's no figuring them out now," Eddy said, sincerely expressing his failure. "Nevertheless, I got to reading, and I stumbled on a collection of articles published by the Huffington Press online. They were articles written by teenage girls and written about their experiences, feelings, and opinions of sex, almost like we were assigned to do here. That was very helpful to start forming my own opinions, and even though they departed a bit from what I had written down from my dad, I was able to nail down what I think and believe. Really, if I could present the pros and cons side by side, I think it paints a fuller picture, but anyway, here's the benefits to having sex on mutual terms," Eddy said, gripping the lectern and referencing his notes. "There're three things I've found. There's my interest in having sex, there's my interest to being in a reliable relationship, and there's babes, I mean babies."

The class laughed.

"If I'm interested in having sex, which I am, and a girl is interested in having sex for the experience or fun of it, there's consent. I feel this is the time of life to find consenting partners and to experiment for the fun of it. Yet, there are three problems with this kind of behavior, but they help get to my other point if you don't mind," Eddy said, looking for and getting a nod of permission from the corner. "Babes, I mean babies are one," Eddy hiccupped intentionally.

The class snickered again.

"But with babies there's contraception, like condoms, which makes sex sound a lot less scary for everyone involved, including parents," Eddy said and referenced his notes again. "Number two isn't a problem for the abstinence-people, but there seems to be a very real emotional connection that happens when you have sex which everybody seemed to describe as 'perfect' in the articles I read. The emotional connection and the flipside of it, which is jealousy, both encourage commitment. This is a pro, but it's also a con, because due to the rapidly changing season of life were in, the relationships can be just as rapidly changing, which means there's more likely a chance of breaking up, and hence more chance of this negative emotion of jealousy," Eddy said, trying to sound logical. Seeing that he was losing the focus of the class, he turned around to the whiteboard and picked up a marker. "And just so you know the type of jealousy I'm talking about, it's J-E-A—LOWSY."

The class politely responded and thanked Eddy for his cleverness by lending him more of their attention.

"Nevertheless thirdly, there's the problem of sexually transmitted diseases which can be mostly minimized from what I've read and can mostly be treated if you come down with

one...of the many. But STDs can't be eliminated altogether,"
Eddy said, tilting his head. "This risk again encourages couples
to stick together, so it's a con but also a pro. So, that's my world
now, but when life settles down after college, these mutual terms
of having sex are more likely to include marriage and children.
This is the time of life I think my dad and most adults are talking
about when they talk about having sex or not having sex. It's
the time that companionship naturally leads to a single partner,
which becomes highly rewarding, and it's the time that having
many sexual partners becomes only more and more risky. So,
that's my opinion and my reasons. Should I write them
somehow up here?" Eddy asked, turning around to face the
whiteboard.

"Yes, applause everyone," Steven instructed. "Cassidy, you're
next."

Eddy wrote, "Perfect fit for my season of life."

*--- Great Gravitations: Journal page twenty-eight, after three post-school
jelly-roll snacks had disappeared and I had reclused myself to the twisted
covers of my bed.*

Cassidy made abstinence sure sound a lot more appealing than
my sex talk, and I know my mother would say an *amen* to that.
Though, something I said must have resonated with her too
because she came up after class and told me that she felt a lot
more comfortable about the topic of sex after listening to me
and that she was going to look up the Huffington Press articles
when she got home. I'm glad she seemed to get something out
of it because the only two things I heard over the next two
hallway breaks were: 'Eddy is having sex' and 'Eddy thinks
everybody should be having sex'. Two false statements, mind
you, that could easily be fixed by inserting the word *wants*. Eddy
WANTS to have sex. Eddy thinks everybody who WANTS to
have sex should be having sex. Well, nix the latter statement; it
doesn't make any sense and only proves where my mind is right
now. But at least people weren't feeling sorry for me anymore.
Besides, and my hand is starting to jitter, that's when—

*--- An hour earlier, after the final Monday school bell, the hallways were
rapidly clearing and were nearly empty.*

"So, I hear you want to have sex now?"

"Yes, thank you. I'm not actually having sex; I merely want to. Melanie! Woah! The last person I was expecting," Eddy said, flipping out with enough surprise in his knees that he could have dunked a basketball without a running start.

"Would you prefer somebody else?"

"No, gosh no. I've had a crush on you for like a year," Eddy said, scratching his head and diverting his gaze like he was watching his favorite two marbles roll across the floor, one to the toes of Melanie's shoes and the other to the threshold of the school office.

"Well, you're unabashedly honest. A crush, huh? I don't know if this will actually work out then," Melanie thought out loud and rocked curiously side to side. Melanie's hair splashed over her head and onto her right shoulder like the curl and spray of a Hawaiian wave. Except rather than being a wave of blue, her hair was the golden color of a sunlit beach.

"Well, if Melanie can't work it out, I sure hope Eddy can eventually," Eddy said, fighting a sudden and hopeless battle against the speed of his heart.

"You seemed to have it all pretty figured out today in class...more than I do," Melanie testified honestly, straight-arming her jean-pant pocket with her secretive hand. Her youthful motion, at least to Eddy, brought her closer to earth than he had ever thought possible. For this girl, to Eddy, that could stare him level in the eye with a stare that could put a tidal wave in the ocean, lived on the moon.

"Are you walking home?" Eddy asked, his words escaping like a rogue toucan from a zoo.

"No, I'm about to skip back to Scott here in a minute. But...you're not going to get all creepy on me if I ask you a question. Are you?"

"I only get creepy after two questions, so you should be good," Eddy said, trying to loosen his shoulders without looking like he was in gym class.

Melanie looked at Eddy with a thought in her head, a thought that then made her pull open her gravitational smile. "Scott and I got in an argument over these last two breaks about you," Melanie said, deciding that she'd go for it. "He thinks your sexually inexperienced ideas are dumb, but I have a different opinion. Plus, I think he wants to have sex with some other chick," Melanie explained, lowering her armor-piercing eyes. "Anyways, I bet him that your sex is better than his...sex. So, my question is: do you have it in you to settle our bet?" Melanie asked, moving one hand behind her back and the other irresistibly behind her head.

"Yes," Eddy said, having no explanation or reason for his answer.

"Yes! Scott is so going to lose," Melanie said, pulling her fist down as if she'd won already.

"Wait, your betting...sorry, it just hit me. You're betting on me!" Eddy said, his eyelids suffering a mild heart attack.

"You said it yourself; sex loses its luster after a while, and we've been having sex for a while. Scott's just too full of himself to admit that he could be better at it."

"But," Eddy said, anxious to speak his claustrophobic thought. "I need permission from him because it sounds like you're wanting me to invade his space."

"Sure. Hold on," Melanie said and dialed a favorited number on her phone. "Hey, Scott. You're so going down on this one. I have our bet-buster right here, asking for your permission, so here he is," Melanie said and handed Eddy the call with a proud thrust.

"Scott, tell me you're not seriously handing out your girlfriend," Eddy said, and checked Melanie's kindled and observant eyes.

"Yeah, go bang her; then tell her to come whimpering back when she wants great sex again."

"He says he wants you to come whimpering back when you lose," Eddy relayed, vainly covering the phone for comedic effect.

"You can tell him to get ready to meet my dad."

"She says her dad is going to love you," Eddy relayed back to Scott.

"Whatever. Have fun learning how to put a condom on," Scott said and hung up the phone.

Now about Scott: Scott's shoulders were stout enough and his face mature enough to convince both genders of the student body that he was the alpha male by default. But since the student body was a far howl from being a wolfpack, it should also be told, if not obvious, that Scott equally repelled many. This repelling could easily be traced back to the fact that he mustered most of his laughs from his following fellows by way of his off-colored remarks and his teetering threats to random targets, some threats as simple as a twist of his dark, plain-yet-bold eyes and eyebrows. In the scheme of this biased description, I will admit that his looks and attitude, though of mixed reception, were bold enough to allure Melanie and somehow tame enough to win and keep her acceptance. He was someone you either were pandering to or you avoided.

The phone was disconnected for a good three count before Eddy reacted to Scott's sarcastic encouragement, "Yeah, I think if he's looking for a vacation, we need to decide where we should go on yours."

"My place, tonight. Sneak around back, and I'll let you in through my window," Melanie instructed as if she had rehearsed her answer.

"Yeah, two things. One, if you're pitting my sexual capabilities against Scott's, Eddy's sex will not be at Eddy's best tonight, and two, you do know that I haven't had sex before," Eddy clarified as he returned Melanie's tele-device. "That last one is a hanging question."

"Hah, dweeb. I haven't had sex with you before either, so we're even," Melanie bragged then laughed.

"Dinner will happen at my house tonight though."

"See, that's moving from fun to creepy."

"Oh, no, no, no. Creepy only happens if you ask me another question," Eddy objected and slid his burning hands into his pockets.

"Okay, what time? ...Nope, I don't want you turning zombie on me. Tell me the time you want me to be there," Melanie said, censoring her question. Mirroring Eddy's posture, she slid both of her hands into her pockets and moved her shoulders the way Cassidy had done earlier when she had approached him.

"Six o'clock, and I'll pick you up. Or my mom and I will," Eddy promised. "Are you allergic to anything?"

"Only viper venom."

"Hah, and Melanie," Eddy said.

"It's Mel, and I'm calling you Eddy, because Ed sounds too blah."

Eddy took a step closer, looking for permission to touch her. Discerning no resistance, he uncovered his fevering hand and placed it on her shoulder. "You have the most attractive figure," Eddy complimented and stepped away toward the school lobby.

"Pretty eyes would be more normal!" Melanie called out and watched Eddy stop and retrace one of his four steps.

"I can't handle your eyes yet. There are no words in my vocabulary to do them justice," Eddy said, facing Melanie as he backed away from her. He memorized all the colors of her beauty as he retreated.

Melanie stood privately intimidated for a moment, twitching twice at the same thought. After Eddy disappeared with his own handsome beam of joy around the corner of the lobby, she walked to the back of the school where the pandering pack and her boyfriend often parked and hung out after dismissal.

--- *A sparse moment later, Eddy had unnecessarily returned to his locker and had walked back to the front exit of the school.*

"So, I'm hearing rumors about you," Alexis greeted, having waited for Eddy outside at the top of the school steps.

"Alexis, what are you waiting around here for?" Eddy asked, slowing to let Alexis join him.

"I figured you needed protection on your walk home."

"Uh, yeah, company would be great too if you have some of that to spare," Eddy said and continued walking off the school grounds next to Alexis. Their step count rose and rose, and Alexis seemed readily content with his company being void of further conversation or commentary. Initially, Eddy was thankful for this due to the sheer volume of his singular thought, but then after a while he felt like Alexis might somehow be supernaturally translating his brain waves, or if not, reading the private plans in the red variety of ink being typewritten on his cheeks. "Hey, you want anything from the gas station?" Eddy asked to break the span of silence and looked to see how his offer fell on Alexis's face.

"Twins."

"Twins for two it is," Eddy said and continued walking toward the convenience store. The convenience store sat a hundred paces or so away on the school side of the four-lane road. "I forgot you lived out my way," Eddy said as they reached the store.

"About halfway, I'd say. I've biked by your house with my friends before," Alexis conveyed, following her taller classmate through the door of the shop.

"Oh, is that so?" Eddy asked and tossed Alexis a Twins bar before he paid the cashier.

"I waited because I wanted to know why you're being so nice to me all of a sudden when you hadn't even so much as spoken to me before Friday morning," Alexis divulged as she led Eddy out of the shop and nonchalantly continued to walk next to Eddy with her favorite candy.

"You weren't the only girl I ignored. In fact, there was only one girl in my universe that I thought worth talking to before Friday," Eddy said and looked down at Alexis's tan profile once more. "Do you really want to know why?"

"I wasted ten minutes of my time, hoping to find out. So yeah," Alexis said competing with the volume of wind from a passing car that swallowed the beginning of her answer.

"Because you don't look like the porn stars that I was watching daily," Eddy said honestly after hearing her affirmative 'So yeah', and he looked to see how his own disclosure had affected his friend. "The moment I stopped checking out every girl that walked by me like I would a porn star, I started seeing fun cool people that I wanted to be around, to make laugh, to interact with, and to get to know."

"I thought you were hitting on me," Alexis said nervously, pushing her long, straight, and nearly black hair over her Native American ear.

"Well, I learned fast: you don't hit on a judo master."

After accepting his humor with a short puff, Eddy and Alexis carried on in silence, letting the squares of sidewalk pass underneath them as they wound deeper into their neighborhood. These sidewalks on either side of the road were well-aged and many of the squares had shifted out of place like plate tectonics on a small scale. Alexis was obviously thinking, and Eddy occasionally looked, trying to diagnose Alexis's thoughts.

"Is this it?" Eddy asked the obvious as Alexis quietly turned into a driveway. Eddy waved at the person waving in the window. "Who is that?"

"That's my baby sister. Thanks for the company, Ed," Alexis said, turning to walk backwards without slowing her gait.

"See you tomorrow!"

"Bye," Alexis said with a snap of her neck and a dry expression leveling her face.

Chapter Five

"Mom!" Eddy called out after he unlocked and opened the wreath-decorated front door. His house, a red-brick one, came snuggly outfitted with a typical, two-car garage. Snug was a good adjective for the garage. And the garage was sidled up next to a dainty front porch that housed a dainty table and two dainty chairs. The snug- and daintiness of these two spaces had never mattered to Eddy, and it would be true to say that he had never entertained a use for either...either. Once inside, Eddy rashly kicked off his school shoes toward the first corner. "Hi, Kristy. Is Mom working today?"

"No, she should be upstairs," Kristy informed, glancing up from her silver-framed reading glasses.

Eddy turned around to see Cynthia appear in the sunlit area at the top of the staircase.

"Hey, Mom, I invited a girl over for dinner before I asked if it was okay. Is that okay?" Eddy asked, watching his mom hold the railing of the staircase as she descended. Eddy noticed the swelling around her eyes.

"A girlfriend over for dinner, you say?"

"Well, a girl I'm interested in," Eddy admitted and saw Kristy turn again with interest.

"That's fine so long as she doesn't stay too late."

"Awesome!"

"What do you think she would like to eat?" Cynthia asked, moving to the kitchen to get a glass of water.

"Nothing fancy. I asked her, and she said that she wasn't allergic to anything."

"I could run out and get us pizzas," Kristy butted in thoughtfully and saw Eddy nod with approval. "What time should I have them here?"

"I told her dinner at six, so I'll leave here in about an hour and a half to go get her and walk her over."

"I'll drive you if you want," Eddy's mom offered and sipped on the water she had poured from the refrigerator.

"Wow, that would be great!" Eddy said, unable to contain his pleasure.

"Where does she live?" Cynthia asked, pulling up the loose sleeves of her light floral blouse.

"I have her address upstairs. I just have to find it."

"Well, let me know, and we can figure out a time to leave."

Kristy looked at Cynthia gladly, and Cynthia finally caught her gaze after Eddy had bolted youthfully up the stairs to his room. Cynthia hardly withheld her grin and then shared a laugh with Kristy over their mutual observation.

--- After a nearly hazardous hour of preparation upstairs with countless dashes between the bathroom mirror and Eddy's closet, Cynthia walked out to the garage with Eddy.

"So, how long have you liked this girl? And what's her name?" Cynthia asked as she pulled out of the driveway right on time.

"Since middle school, and it's Melanie."

"So, there's high hopes for this one then," Cynthia concluded and looked over at Eddy as if she had asked a question.

"Yes! Dad sat me down recently and explained a few things that helped me see girls differently. I sure wouldn't be having you drive me to her house right now if I hadn't changed my perspective," Eddy said, liking the chance to talk about his dad with his mom.

"Oh, and what did he explain?" Cynthia asked and gave Eddy a chance to think as she put the car into forward motion and steered around a bend in their side street.

"He said that I needed to stop looking at girls like I was looking at pornography. And then he told me it would be in my best interest to stop looking at pornography altogether. And then he told me that, as far as it goes with relationships, I need to start treating girls like I was doing everything in their best interest. It kind of goes along with the loving your neighbor philosophy that you talk about on stage."

Though Eddy had spoken without interruption, he had thought pensively through each new string of words at each stop sign that the car had happened upon along their short journey.

"That's pretty profound coming from Max," Cynthia said shortly after the end of Eddy's space-filled discourse and revealed in a glance that her eyes had welled up again with tears.

"I'm sorry, I shouldn't have brought up Dad," Eddy apologized.

"What? No, no. I couldn't be happier right now, hearing you speak so wisely. Girls cry sometimes when they're happy," Cynthia said, blurring the real cause for her tears with a rather true platitude as she crossed into the subdivision per the GPS instructions. "I know it's kind of confusing, but please tell me anything about Max. I'll let you know if I ever need a break from your memories of him," Cynthia said, raising her eyebrows to acknowledge her son's growing posture. Eddy's posture grew in intensity like a snail reading a climactic novel until Melanie's house came into view. It was an old house, where the pitch of the house's roof was barely steep enough to encourage water runoff, and its vinyl siding had, at some time past, acquired a small collection of mildew. Though the landscaping beds and full-grown bushes had long been released back to the wild, the small yard of green weeds mixed with grass had not been left uncut for more than a week. The front windows on the right of the house were pressed with white blinds, and the short cement staircase to the mushroom-colored front door had an illuminated porchlight to the left of it. Cynthia had no idea what to expect from this jack-in-the-box abode, but she hid her opined judgement for sake of her son's enthusiasm and obvious nerves. Getting nervous herself, Cynthia watched Eddy walk up to the door and wait like he was changing his mind. Then with unified knuckles, he knocked. At the point of his knocking, her attention to peripheral details was lost because the door opened, and a girl stepped out to meet her son. Like a T-shirt caught on a nail, her sown together lips ripped at their seam. The girlfriend's clothing, her golden wave of hair, how she scrunched her shoulders in response to something that Eddy had said, all of it, Cynthia scoured. Consuming fire in her eyes unfairly spread from the height to the foot of the clearly attractive girl, trying to find some flaw to privately judge, but her judgement had little time to burn. She watched Eddy offer Melanie his arm and saw Melanie visibly soften when she took it.

The young couple's linkage slowed them down and forced them to sync their steps to keep from bumping into each other's shoulders. In detail, Cynthia could see her son introducing her as they got closer to the car which brought an unconscious beam to her face. And before she knew it, she was talking with Melanie as her son found his way around to the other side of the backseat.

"Hi, I'm Cynthia."

"Hi, Cynthia. You're Eddy's mom. Right? Not his aunt?" Melanie clarified. "I'm Mel by the way, Melanie Westin."

"I am, and his Aunt Kristy is over tonight also. I'm so glad you could join us for dinner."

"Mom, is it normal to be this nervous when you're sitting with a pretty girl?" Eddy blurted out, causing his mom to laugh and Melanie to blush a little.

"Do you want me to answer that?" Cynthia asked, unsure of her son's intention.

"No, but I would like to say, Mom, that you look stunning in that dress. You can't appreciate it while she's driving, but wait till she stands up," Eddy complimented and turned to Melanie to convince her.

"I thought you would be complimenting me," Melanie stated curiously, making brief eye contact with the driver.

"Oh, is it time for that already?" Eddy asked. "Hold on." Eddy reached into his pocket and removed a pocket-sized book. Flipping it open to the first tab, he said, "Your eyes are pulchritudinous." Eddy looked up for feedback and saw Melanie's face wiggle and contort before he continued, "Nope, that's not it. Okay, honestly the only word I've found that almost begins to describe you this evening, and specifically your eyes, is resplendent," Eddy said, hoping his mannerisms would be taken the right way.

"Resplendent, I can bite on that," Melanie said and slid her hand across the bottom of the back seat to let Eddy know that he could hold it. With the connection, silence fell upon the car like it does with a table of guests after food is delivered, and this food was truly delicious.

Enjoying herself and her play with Eddy's thumb and wanting to vocalize it in some way, Melanie mimicked Eddy and boldly asked, "So, Mrs. Kraft, what did your son do to get ready for tonight's dinner?"

Cynthia sat up to attention and looked in the rearview mirror to make sure the question was directed to her. "Eddy? Well, he took a shower and ordered pizza," Cynthia said concisely.

"And also, I brushed my teeth and read a one-hundred-and-fifty-seven-page thesaurus," Eddy included. "But, figuring out which pizza you would like was definitely the most stressful part."

"Why didn't you...just tell him to ask?" Melanie asked, redirecting her question to the driver.

"Oh, he did, didn't you? I told him to."

"You know, it turns out that I don't have your phone number," Eddy admitted, looking at Melanie to see if she would then have any intention of giving it to him.

"Here, dial in your mom's phone number," Melanie volunteered, pulling her small phone out of her purse and handing it to Eddy.

"My mom's or mine?" Eddy queried, thinking he may have misheard.

"Your mom's," Melanie repeated, looking at Cynthia's dress and comparing it to her selection of clothing.

Cynthia perked up with interest, and her auburn bob shifted a few times, telling the rear seat passenger that she was glancing at her in the rearview mirror.

Eddy did as Melanie requested and scratched his cheekbone as he handed back Melanie's phone.

Melanie readily saved and then called Cynthia's number and listened to the phone simultaneously ring and buzz in the front seat.

Familiar with the technique of transferring phone numbers, but still thinking it strange, Cynthia set her curious eyes back to driving.

As Cynthia turned the car into their driveway, Melanie turned with the phone to her ear and saw Eddy looking over at her with an equal bout of curiosity. Savoring his expression like the touch of his thumb, she began at the prompt, "Hi, Mrs. Kraft, this is Melanie Westin. I just wanted to thank you so much for picking me up and having me over for dinner tonight. You have a wonderful son, and I had a really great time," Melanie said in the most convincing tone, and then she hung up. The silence fell in the car, hotter than before, like they were trapped in a humid, stuffy room, and the fact that Cynthia had shut off the engine only amplified the heaviness of the atmosphere.

Beside herself, Cynthia was flabbergasted and had to forcibly interrupt her eyes that had returned to their staring in the rearview mirror.

"How do you know that you'll have a great time tonight?" Eddy fairly asked, bumbling to fill the silence that had already lingered too long.

"I don't think you can mess this one up, Eddy," Melanie responded and finally let go of his hand.

Eddy jumped out of the car after the encouragement and commenced the cordial walk into the house where he introduced Melanie to Kristy and gave his polite guest a brief tour of their two stories. After the amateur tour, when Eddy had left to wash up and Kristy was out of the room setting the table, Cynthia paused her busy hands and said, "Melanie, thank you for that message. I'm glad Eddy has a good friend to help him through this hard time."

"He seems to be killing it at school. You should've heard his presentation in health class. Is he sick or something?"

"Oh, I'm sorry. I thought you knew already. His dad passed away of a heart attack last Friday."

"Last Friday!?" Melanie gasped. "That little bugger...keeping secrets."

Cynthia pleasantly absorbed Melanie's honest yet playful reaction while finding an excuse on the counter to hide her returned silence.

"What'd I miss?" Eddy asked, walking back into the room and looking between the blank faces. "Oh, I'm busted, aren't I? Mel, I should've told you that I've had a lifelong obsession with models...airplane models, tanks, old cars, and such."

"No," Melanie laughed as her face morphed with concern. "You didn't tell me your dad passed away."

"That was on the agenda, I promise. Are you hungry?" Eddy responded off guard, barely keeping enough air in his windpipe to redirect the topic.

Throughout the next broken waves of conversation while pizza was served and consumed, Eddy felt the dagger of worry

stabbing his bones, worry that Melanie's likable presence and her
heart-mending concern would horribly pass away like his dad's
sudden departure.

--- *Despite his jostled thoughts, with pizza and dinner conversations
enjoyed, Melanie accepted Eddy's invitation to sit on the front porch.*

"Tell me about my resplendent eyes again," Melanie said as
Eddy flicked on the porchlight from behind his date.

"Here. Take a seat," Eddy invited, pointing to the set of chairs
that were separated by their miniature outdoor table. "I need
some inspiration; hold on," Eddy excused and sat down opposite
Melanie to gaze into her eyes. Her eyes were purely arresting,
eyes that, if a watchmaker could have captured their hue and
pattern for the backdrop of a simple timepiece, would render the
timekeeper timeless or anyone with a schedule late. Eddy was
arrested by this thought and another equally pleasant one, but his
tongue was captured as much as his admiration.

Melanie looked back into Eddy's eyes, enticed by his
proposition. Though hard to judge exactly under the warm
porch lights and the array of orange and pink color crossing the
sky, she could tell Eddy's eyes were a darker color like her own.

"How do I describe what I'm feeling?" Eddy rhetorically asked
and took a deep breath.

Melanie watched him slowly exhale and said, "Try."

"Give me your hand."

Before she completely curled her hand around his, she moved
in to kiss him.

When she finally let go of her kiss, Eddy said, "Butterflies, two
resplendent butterflies too fascinating to take your eyes away
from."

"That's a little better," Melanie said and saw Eddy eyeing
another kiss. Melanie reclined back into her seat and started
twirling her thumb around Eddy's.

Reading the cues, Eddy did likewise and asked, "What do you
like about your dad?"

"That he doesn't impede my space. Tell me what you liked
about yours."

Eddy thought for a moment and said, "That he cared enough
to tell me I was headed down the wrong road and trusted me
enough to tell me how to go about getting on the right one."

"Sex."

"Is that a question?"

"No. I don't want you to turn into Frankenstein because I want to kiss you again."

"I was just kidding about the two-question thing."

"Well, I'm serious," Melanie said, looking over to judge Eddy's comprehension.

Eddy totally understood and happily made himself available.

--- Great Expectations: The middle of journal page twenty-nine, written much later that evening under my nightstand lamp, after my lights had already been out for two flips of my normally comfortable pillow.

It's amazing to me how you don't have to think while you're kissing, and yet you're still very much having a meaningful conversation. Melanie's lips taste like honey, and her tongue is sweet. And I know it's gross to think about, but it's the same feeling as eating an entire box of Mike & Kie Fruits, where you know the box is empty, but you reach back in anyway, hoping to find one more taste of bliss.

--- Back on the porch nearly three hours earlier, without noticing that the sun had set, Melanie and Eddy still had found no reason to conclude their evening. After teasing each other through another round of kissing, the front door opened.

Cynthia walked out on the porch to ask the pair, that she had thrice caught kissing from inside, if they were ready to retire.

Melanie looked relaxed and at ease while keeping her eyes on Eddy's. "I'm ready," she said calmly.

"That was—"

"Shhh," Melanie hushed and suppressed a laugh.

"Let me get her things, and we'll be ready," Eddy said, finally turning around to address his mother.

Eddy rose to his feet, and before long, Cynthia had the car pointed toward Melanie's house.

"How long were you married, Mrs. Kraft?"

"Eighteen-and-a-half years. How about your parents, Mel?" Cynthia asked, smiling at her son, who now sat kiddy-corner her for the return trip.

"My dad says that he and my mother weren't together for much longer than her pregnancy and says that I only met her when she gave birth to me."

"Oh. Well, at least you didn't have to divide your love any," Cynthia gently remarked to apologize.

"Can you do that? Okay, where did you give birth to Eddy?" Melanie asked, smirking as she leaned toward the center console.

"London. What was the longest you've ever grown out your hair?" Cynthia rebounded.

"Down to my butt. Which wasn't too long because I was short in elementary school. Do you have any tattoos that Eddy doesn't know about?" Melanie asked, enjoying both Cynthia's attention and her motherly candidness.

"No, thankfully. I'm too squeamish around needles. Best place to buy ice cream in the city?"

"Right there. And why is Eddy being so quiet?" Melanie asked cleverly.

"I don't know; ask him," Cynthia replied, looking in the rearview mirror at her son, who sat eyeing the girl sitting next to him.

Melanie looked at Eddy, who returned her gaze. "Why...are you being so quiet? Eddy?" Melanie emphasized softly.

"It's raining information around here, and it's all about you. I'm hanging on for dear life. Have you ever wanted to be a cheerleader?" Eddy asked, spouting the first question that popped into his mind.

"I was one in seventh grade and didn't like it," Melanie said and looked for a moment at Eddy's nice face. "Do you have a treasure box hidden somewhere that you keep your secrets inside of?"

"I used to have a digital one, but the things inside of it scare me now. So, no," Eddy answered, smiling more than he had been. "Would you pull an all-nighter to make sure you completed a project on time?"

"I don't procrastinate."

"Ever?"

"Do I look like a procrastinator?" Melanie asked and enjoyed seeing the turmoil grow on Eddy's face.

"I plead the fifth."

"Oh!" Cynthia and Melanie sang together in delight while Melanie squeezed Eddy's hand in warm consolation.

"You got me, fair and square. May I walk you up?" Eddy asked before the car stopped in the driveway.

"No, I'll be fine."

"I'd like to," Eddy doubled down.

"I know you want...okay. Come on, get my door," Melanie said with attractive aggravation, quickly retracting her stubbornness to avoid a needless scene. As she put her purse on her lap, she said, "Thank you, Mrs. Kraft, for letting me enjoy your family tonight."

"It was all our pleasure, Mel," Cynthia welcomed.

"Am I that easy to read?" Eddy asked as he closed Melanie's door.

"I had a wonderful time, Eddy," Melanie said, ignoring the question. "You're just a friend dropping me off. Okay?" Melanie said, disclosing her predicament.

"Sorry; got it."

"You're complicating my life, creep."

"Ouch. Arrow through heart," Eddy responded, fishing for some sign of sarcasm.

"My dad thinks I'm out studying."

"Well, you kind of were studying," Eddy offered. "Creep is harsh. Can we pick another word?"

"It was your word."

"Still, I want you to be real when I show you affection, so was creep real or was my three-hour interview with you real?" Eddy asked, following Melanie's implied instruction and keeping his distance.

"I'm trying to keep things real, Eddy. But I have to go back to school tomorrow with your tender affections floating around in my brain while playing happy runner-up with Scott."

"Then leave him!"

"I might. Goodnight."

"Goodnight, Mel. Thanks for studying with me," Eddy said when Melanie had opened her front door, and he thought he saw the same look, the irresistible gleam, that he had first witnessed on their kissing porch. He coveted confirmation to know if it was, but the door closed, leaving him battling with his hope and wonder.

Eddy walked back to where his mom was waiting with the car engine running, and he climbed in, feeling like an acidic flow of ash was threatening to rise up from the throat of a waking volcano. However, one look at his mother told him that his present worries were better suited for another time and place.

"Eddy Kraft!"

"Yes, Mom?" Eddy asked, trying not to tense up.

"You were dashing! I don't know who taught you to do all that, but I'm really impressed," Cynthia said, pulling the car out onto the road for their return trip. "You gave Melanie a dream date for the price of a pizza box and a taxi ride. You were witty and fun. And I don't know who had the better time, Kristy and me, or Mel and you!"

Apprehensively encouraged, Eddy replied, "Thanks. You and Dad taught me how to flirt like that."

"Well, you've refined whatever skills your father and I have demonstrated," Cynthia said sincerely and then fought with her contemplative expression. "When we were in college, we would have called you a heartbreaker," Cynthia spilled. "Because as you see, as dashing and flirtatious as you are, you can manipulate even the most discerning girls into doing things they wouldn't agree to otherwise."

"So, it's not all a compliment is what you're saying," Eddy concluded.

"No. What I'm saying is have you thought about what happens when you start flirting with two or three or ten or twenty other girls at school and they all want your exclusive attention?" Cynthia asked and paused so that Eddy might reflect on her words. "They go home and cry because they can't compete with the prettier girl that you choose to be more endearing to," Cynthia continued, trying immensely to keep her tone positive. "A heartbreaker," Cynthia consolidated, breathing as she considered making a dangerous point. She stopped but decided it was necessary. "All a heartbreaker would have to do to pressure a girl like Mel to go farther than she's sexually comfortable would be to start flirting with girl B. And once girl A has given all she has, what then?" Cynthia asked. Immediately realizing that her question was unfair, she continued, "That's why I see it as so important to date intentionally with a girl's best interest at heart."

"Wait. Dad used that phrase," Eddy said, using his intrigue to hide any expression of guilt.

"Well, good for him. He also helped me write my book. I also hear it termed *stirring up emotions*," Cynthia said as she put the car in park in their driveway.

"So, what does a guy do when he wants to have sex with girl A? And what if I really like flirting?"

"You have to learn to look at the bigger picture and decide to have control of your desires in the moment," Cynthia said, relieved at not seeing a rebellious wedge in her son's eyebrows.

"So, celibacy now, and marriage later?"

"It's all a balance, but the *you're-young, experiment-all-you-can* mentality can really hurt people emotionally and physically."

"How do you practice then?" Eddy asked and saw his mom look at him judgingly. Nevertheless, Eddy dared to continue, "If you're not going to risk *stirring up emotions* in this time of life while marriage isn't an option, how do you engage with girls?"

Cynthia saw that her son missed her inference and said, "Carefully. Be careful with your words and be careful with your relationships. Don't invite girls into your bedroom."

"What if I want to go into their bedroom and have sex because their attractive?"

"Sex isn't just an emotionless act for most people. It can be, but that's far-far-far from the norm. Like when Mel called you a creep," Cynthia said and stopped her point, recognizing her slip.

Eddy gave away all plausible deniability when he looked at his mom the way he did. Then as his brain sped to Hong Kong and back, he forcibly blinked while trying to compute all the implications of his mother having overheard their private conversation. "Ahhh, I had this all figured out before you started talking!" Eddy said with exasperation. "What would make you proud of me, Mom?" Eddy asked, realizing his words also had implications.

"For you to find a girl to love for ten-thousand and forevermore days, and to raise a houseful of grand babies."

"That sounds a lot easier to accomplish than me trying to mitigate and tend all the emotions of every girl I encounter.

Would you be proud of me if I kept kissing Melanie and have other friends that are girls at the same time?" Eddy honestly asked. "And no plead the fifth."

"I'm sorry, my childhood memories are flooding my mind, Eddy," Cynthia said to explain her sudden swelling of emotion. "I most desperately hated a boy in high school for breaking my heart, and for years, I've wanted to instill values in you so that my own son wouldn't become like that boy. And here you are, more handsome and cunning than ever, making your own choices. All I can say is find a girl like Mel, that cherishes family, and pursue her with everything that's in here," Cynthia said, touching her chest. "And protect her and any child she might give you with every muscle that's in here," Cynthia continued, gripping her son's shoulder.

Eddy wiped one of his own eyes with his sleeve and said, "Mom, I think you're trying to make me appreciate our talk."

Cynthia laughed and opened her door to retreat into their red-brick castle—snug, dainty, and plain though it was.

Chapter Six

Umm. This is the part where Melanie and I have sex. So, if you're not interested in all the private details, just skip ahead to the next chapter, or entry, or whatever you call these things.

--- *On day three of our sexual educational instruction, impressively so, Steven Kloomsfield breached the dam that let loose every student and their bottled-up opinions on the subject.*

"Abstinence would be boring. You can write that one up on the board," Scott said to the teacher.

"If that's your idea, you can write it," Steven Kloomsfield responded. "What else? If you have questions for Cassidy, Ed, or me from yesterday, now's the time to ask," Steven said, addressing the class as he waited for Scott to move from his seat.

"I feel like with abstinence, you're missing out on your youth," a student replied. "Like you're sitting on your hands till you're too old to date."

"Missing out. Okay, come up and write it," Steven instructed, holding out an erasable pen.

"Do you think that at some certain age you hit an *age* wall, and you're not allowed to date people anymore?" Sarah inquired harshly.

"If you get married, there is," Cassidy defended.

"See, boring," Scott added. "Marriage restricts you to boredom."

"And divorce can get messy," Melanie added, rising to her feet to obediently record her response.

"But wouldn't having open sex be just as messy as divorce is when it comes to having children?"

"Write that up there, Cassidy," Steven Kloomsfield instructed.

"Not necessarily, because a girl wouldn't go off contraception until she understands the likelihood that she'd be raising the kid alone," came a different student's attempt at a logical counterpoint.

"That's still a single parent raising a child though," Eddy said.

"Write it," Steven said, tossing a marker to Eddy.

"You can get STDs during premarital sex," another student pointed out.

"You can get STDs while you're married, when you get bored and sleep around," Scott added, smirking.

"I'm going to term that infidelity and write that up here for you, Scott, because that's a good point. And though sexually transmitted diseases are significantly less likely if two people wait to have sex till they're married, they can still acquire certain STDs even if they do remain faithful to each other," Steven explained.

"So, there's STDs in every column?" Sarah remarked, hoping the teacher would clarify the surprising information.

"Yes, but you're much more likely to get them on this end of the scale, and that's just due to shear statistics. We'll talk about STDs in greater detail over the following week, believe me."

"You don't need to worry about contraception or what birth control can do to your body with abstinence," Cassidy said after a moment of silence.

"That's true; here, I got it," Steven said, and moved two steps over to also add the converse under the middle ground and open sex columns. "Though, I will say that many married couples do end up investing in birth control to better plan their pregnancy."

"Not for Catholics," a student objected, shooting his hand up and down without being called upon.

"Not for Catholics, you're right. Any religion will have its expectations governing what we're talking about today, and if you don't know what your religion believes, you shouldn't hesitate to ask your minister."

"What about jealousy," Melanie said. "Open sex and the open sex part of the middle ground don't take into account the very real emotion of jealousy."

"There's also guilt that goes along with compromising your standards," Cassidy said and stood up with Melanie to return to the board.

"That's why you don't have sex with ugly people."

"Hey, hey, Scott. You're done answering."

"Just saying," Scott defended, crossing his arms as he balanced the two front legs of his chair in the air.

"People looking and hoping for a relationship will often compromise their personal standards just to get or to keep the relationship. You promise yourself that you won't cross a certain line, and then you stoop at the critical moment because you can't see or you forget about the bigger picture."

"That's a good summary, Ed," Steven complimented as he assessed the jumble of answers on the whiteboard. "Good!"

--- Eddy watched the next two periods disappear, and after the expiration of his final class, history, he jumped into the hallway with his brown searching eyes.

Eddy rounded the corner, spotted, and in a few running steps, caught up to Melanie, who was walking through the lobby alone. "Are bets still on?"

"Woah, look at you, all energetic," Melanie said, raising her positively magnetic cheeks without slowing down. "Didn't your dad just pass away?"

"Yeah."

"Well, you look like you recovered quickly," Melanie said as Eddy pushed open the front door of the school.

"I'll cry tomorrow; don't worry," Eddy said, stepping along with Melanie in the direction of her house. An extra push of wind from a delivery truck raised the pressure on Eddy's backpack and curled Melanie's hair downwind over her shoulders. Letting other boosts of wind freely push them down the road, they walked along side by side. When they turned the corner onto a cross street, the tall corner building obstructed the wind so that their ability to hear returned.

"You have till 5:30 to prove you're right, by the way," Melanie said, continuing the conversation where she had left it before their stretch of windy walking.

"Is there any way you'd make it not a bet?" Eddy asked in response to the conundrum he was feeling, knowing exactly what Melanie meant.

"Why, have your standards risen?" Melanie asked coldly and watched Eddy's elbows shrivel. When Eddy seemed like he was going to dodge her question, she continued, "Bet's still on. I'm still with Scott."

Eddy thought for about twenty more paces and decided. Then with his fresh decision still spooling in his head like a raucous jet engine roaring for takeoff, he consciously returned to Melanie and announced, "Well then, I guess that means I have two-and-a-half hours left to show you how much fun you can have with Eddy Kraft. May I have your hand, mademoiselle?"

"Eddy, I don't speak French," Melanie answered, hiding her nerves behind her joke and slapping her hand into Eddy's.

"Isn't that where lovers go? To Paris? Aren't I the favored one, who gets to tag along on your vacation?"

"My house?"

"Now that sounds like prime real estate that has real-life ambience of home away from home. But first we're stopping at the best ice cream shop in the city."

"Really?!" Melanie asked with surprise like a girl that had just received parental permission to attend the verboten school dance.

"And I don't even know what it's called."

"Bunny Two Scoops!"

"What a fun-promising name!" Eddy said, feeling alive again at the sight of Melanie's wonderful expression.

"Did you shower today?"

"On my first day of sex. Are you kidding? I brushed my teeth and tongue like on every break after lunch. The convenience store had condoms and lube, so I bought those. And what else did I do to get ready?" Eddy asked himself and pushed into the ice cream shop. The rush of frozen air hit the students in the face like an igloo door had been flung open, and they playfully weaved right to the front of the empty waiting queue. "We're living large today, so get whatever you want," Eddy invited and then listened to Melanie's order of a larger-than-life-sized ice cream cone after shifting her eyes around the overhead menu.

"This place has the best cherry frozen yogurt," Melanie said with an infectious giddy spirit.

"Really? I'll have to try some."

"You will."

"I'll have what she's having," Eddy said to the clerk.

"No, he won't. We're sharing."

"We are? We are...sharing," Eddy apologized.

The attendant, slightly humored, stepped away to prepare the oversized order.

"What? You can't share?" Melanie objected, poorly acting the part of a bully with her hiccups of repressed joy. "Huh?" she pushed, nearly touching Eddy's forehead with hers.

"Okay, what you're doing is quite irresistible," Eddy admitted, putting his hand around Melanie's waist as she did the same around his neck.

"It's called seduction," Melanie informed, letting confidence infect her vocal cords.

"Here you go. That'll be nine twenty-five," the attendant said, and watched the girl steal a kiss before she released her boyfriend-of-the-present to pay the charge.

"Two spoons please," Eddy asked when he saw Melanie spin with delight away from the counter holding the toppling waffle cone.

"I'll get this one in line," Melanie interrupted, pulling Eddy away from the counter to show him where the spoons were located.

"Keep the change," Eddy said as he moved out of reach.

"Spoons and napkins please," Melanie instructed, pausing only long enough to let Eddy take hold of two spoons and one napkin from two different dispensers. "Outside."

"Oh, an outdoorsy girl?"

"Yes! And on a beach," Melanie said, focusing on securing herself the first bite of ice cream with her tongue.

"A beach!? Well, we'll need to change our Paris travel plans then. Where to?"

--- *Since ice cream that's at the right temperature is easily consumed and since Bunny Two Scoops was only two streets away from Melanie's house, the couple arrived at their elected destination still plenty ahead of vacation schedule, i.e. ahead of Melanie's dad's get-off-work time.*

"Down the hall to the left. I need to pee," Melanie said and ducked into her hallway bathroom.

Eddy continued and found Melanie's bedroom. The first thing he noticed was that she had made her bed beautifully, unlike his own standard practice. Next, he noticed that she liked pink and liked everything else orderly. The typical childhood stuffed animals lined the dresser and a shear veil fell over the top of the bed. Suddenly his nerves tensed up when he heard the toilet flush. Putting his bag down on the floor neatly by the dresser out of respect, he walked over to a comfortable looking seat in the corner and sat down.

Melanie came down the hallway and tried to act sexy in the door frame.

"Okay, this is going to be awkward as I see you're way more confident with your perfect body than I am. So, if you'll let me be manly for a minute, I'm going to express my sheer and utter fright and then ask you to barter with me."

Melanie rolled her eyes, closed the door, and walked over to kneel in front of Eddy.

"Okay, stop for a second," Eddy said. "Hands off. That's my manliness move," Eddy said nervously and took a breath, seeing he was about to offend Melanie. "Now, I have never in my life undressed a girl or disrobed in front of a girl, so bear with me. That's my sheer and utter fright."

"Which I can fix," Melanie promised as if Eddy had handed her a compliment. Standing up and motioning for Eddy to follow, she intentionally took Eddy's hands and placed them on her chest. "Hold on," Melanie instructed as she reached around and unhooked a clasp from her backside. "Still holding?" Melanie inquired and slid the bra out from the pressure of Eddy's hands.

"That surprisingly worked," Eddy admitted, and seeing his chance, he continued, "Now my bargain is a hard one, but I won't take my pants off until you're satisfied, or you tell me to."

Melanie laughed, "Oh, you don't want to wait around for me to come."

"But that's my point. If you don't feel great, there's no point in me being here. And if it takes hours for you to climax, I'm game with that."

"Really? You don't want anything, and I just get to enjoy myself?"

"Absolutely! Deal?" Eddy confirmed, hoping to close his bargain.

"Okay," Melanie agreed and warned, "Your loss is my gain!" Melanie looked around the room with a new desire. "I just want to be kissed in your arms like last night, just a lot closer."

"Your perfect lips? Gladly."

"Yours aren't too shabby yourself you know. Sit down on the floor against the bed," Melanie instructed, and when he had, she kneeled over his legs.

"Is this closer?" Eddy asked after a few introductory kisses.

"Uh-huh," Melanie said and continued kissing.

Eddy reached up and removed a strand of hair from her cheek and ran the rest of his hand over her ear.

"See you're a natural."

"Kiss me again," Eddy said.

"How'd you put it? Gladly!" Melanie replied, running her own fingers through his hair. "Hang on a second. I remembered something."

"What's that?" Eddy asked as he watched Melanie dismount and walk over to her nightstand.

"You're going to ejaculate soon, virgin," Melanie informed, returning with a condom. "This will make it less messy to clean up. May I?"

"Yes please. I've never seen how to put one on," Eddy admitted, watching Melanie unzip his pants and guide his penis through the folds.

"It's easy. See? Just leave some room for your...your stuff at the tip. Now you can tuck him away or leave him out it's up to you," Melanie said, settling down for a few more kisses. "Now it would be nice if you could get inspired to remove my shirt and massage my girl parts, gently. That would be the equivalent of my hands finding their way into your pants."

"Gladly," Eddy said again, accepting the challenge.

"Scott likes to look, touch, and be done with them, but I could have a forty-minute breast massage every night before bed."

"Do you time that out, or is that your guesstimate?" Eddy asked in his moment to breathe.

"You can," Melanie said looking at Eddy's focus. "Just don't bite them, please."

Eddy nearly winced in disbelief at the invitation.

"See what I mean, you like looking, touching, and kissing for a minute, but then you want to move on. Just massage them like this, and remember the nipple is more sensitive. Just run your finger around it for a couple of minutes. The same thing, just slowly," Melanie said, rolling her neck around to let her hair fall freely behind her back.

"I feel like one of those music makers that has the tuba, drum, and tambourine and plays them all at once," Eddy said, trying his best to obey.

"If you're tired you can stop."

"That's not what I want, but do you want me to?" Eddy expressed and looked for his answer on Melanie's face.

"I'd like to get in the mood on the bed," Melanie answered and shifted in that direction like a feline cat starting the game of follow-the-leader.

"Okay," Eddy said, picking himself up off the floor to watch Melanie pull back the covers.

"What's that for?" Eddy asked, noting a small towel in the center of the bed.

"That's how I got ready for this, this morning," Melanie replied and moved herself into a sleep-like position with her butt on the towel. "I'm surprised, you haven't come yet."

"Don't remind me about it," Eddy warned and re-commenced his massaging her.

"Just something consistent and gentle whether it's your lips or tongue. No!"

"Sorry," Eddy immediately apologized after retracting his touch.

"That felt like your teeth."

"It was my lips," Eddy said honestly.

"Oh," Melanie said and laid her head back down on the pillow. When Eddy retreated, she looked up to see why. "You didn't injure me; I just didn't like it. I really liked what you were doing before," she explained, her inflection melting through Eddy's reaction to her cold snap like a blow dryer on an icicle. "Why don't you straddle me. You'd be more comfortable, and you might even be...able." Melanie stopped her instructing.

After what seemed like an abnormal length of time, Eddy asked, "Are you still awake?"

"Absolutely."

"Cause you look asleep," Eddy said from his position.

"Would you rather me talk your ear off?" Melanie asked sarcastically without feeling the need to open her eyes.

"No, but nibbling my ear sounds good."

"Well then, take your shirt off; this is my favorite part, chest to chest," Melanie said and her face turned on like a gas fireplace as Eddy complied and moved into the enticing position.

"But what can I do for you?" Eddy asked with his ear in nibbling distance.

"Sometimes you just have to wait your turn, but you can always play with my hair," Melanie answered and started nibbling. Laughing, she explained, "I never thought I'd have to say that to a boy. You're weird. In the best kind of way."

Eddy had trouble focusing on Melanie's hair enough to play with it because of Melanie's following delicate dance of touches.

"You sound like a girl coming," Melanie observed after Eddy began having trouble keeping still.

"Are you turned off by how you're making me feel?" Eddy asked to overturn the insult and relaxed with his forehead dug into Melanie's pillow.

"No, it's actually quite arousing. In fact, get off for a second," Melanie instructed and removed the rest of her clothing in one curling motion. "This is the part Scott always calls boring. Feel me and tell me if I'm wet."

"Not particularly," Eddy said, unfamiliar with the female weather gauge.

"Hmm, I thought I would have been by now. Oh well, hand me the tube-looking bottle inside there," Melanie directed, indifferently pointing at a drawer on her night stand.

"This is the lube?" Eddy asked after stretching and wiggling the indicated drawer open.

"For when I'm dry. Sometimes I don't need it at all. It's intuitive. Yes, just like that," Melanie encouraged, relaxing her legs.

"Are you climaxing?"

"No, far from it. The coolness just feels so good," Melanie explained and continued relaxing. "This is where you try different rhythms and ask me what I like best. Then think *massage*, like you did so well before."

"Is this right?" Eddy asked, knowing he was completely guessing.

"Nothing's right and nothing's wrong, so long as you don't pinch or bite me."

"Do you like longer or quicker," Eddy asked again with curiosity.

"You're thinking too much short game. Longer, and don't change the pace, or at least don't let me know that you're changing the pace," Melanie said and put her arm over her face in another posture of sleep.

If they had been cloud watching, another ten minutes of sky would have gone by without any new shapes appearing.

"Do you see why Scott might get bored?" Melanie asked, peaking from under her elbow, but Eddy's touching of her breast silenced her train of thought. More time disappeared.

"Kiss me. No, keep rubbing, and kiss me," Melanie prompted.

Eddy did and felt a drop of sweat roll down his forehead from bending over Melanie for so long. He pressed on, putting pressure on Melanie's lips and massaging as long and as rhythmically as he could manage for still another span of promising sky. After a little rupture and arching in Melanie's back, Eddy asked, "Did you come?"

"No, so close," Melanie breathed and reached her neck up to pull Eddy's lips back down.

Eddy had lost count of the number of similar clouds that had passed, but his hand and back were sore, and his body was to the point that his fatigued muscles would soon no longer support him. Then like he had unleashed the gust front of spring's opening storm, Melanie moved, shook, and wiggled before saying with conviction, "Quickly."

Eddy understood and ripped his clothes off in compliance.

While having a rash debate between watching and imagining, Melanie felt Eddy ignorantly maneuver into position. "That's the wrong hole."

"That's good to know."

"Here," Melanie said, grabbing Eddy's appendage and guiding it into place. This forced Eddy to fall naturally an inch away from her eyes. "Now it's your turn."

Eddy instinctively moved and laid his full body down on Melanie's.

"Or maybe I'm not done...," Melanie said, and her voice regressed back into the pleasing and magnetic sounds of nature.

At her desiring sound, Eddy could no longer hold back what was inside and moved erratically for less than five seconds. After that, all was still, and they lay connected and panting.

"Where did you learn to do that?"

"From you," Eddy complimented, feeling like his thrill was twice as big as Melanie's.

"Why are you smiling at me like that?"

"You know why. Why are you out of breath?"

"Intense," Melanie summarized.

"You're amazing," Eddy said and watched Melanie laugh in agreement.

"And you're still inside of me," Melanie said, crossing her arms behind Eddy's neck.

"I'm still enjoying myself."

"Oh man, that doesn't happen...with," Melanie said, rolling her neck to the side. "That doesn't happen," she repeated and fell quiet.

"That was amazing," Eddy commented again to ignore what felt like the tap of asp teeth hitting his neck and the heat of its poison swelling up the back side of his head. Strung between the receding wave of pleasure and the undertow of Melanie's inferred comparison, Eddy shivered violently once.

"How was your two seconds of pleasure?" Melanie asked without turning back toward him, and a similar convulsion ran down her spine.

"It was amazing!" Eddy said a third time, waiting for Melanie to look at him after her own shiver. Inside, he was violently raising the drawbridge to repel the charge of his crusading conscience.

"You keep saying that, and you're still inside of me."

"Kiss me, and I'll get out," Eddy said, boggling his interpretation of Melanie's distant gaze.

Melanie gave Eddy a less than passionate kiss and stretched her arms out with satisfaction. "That was amazing."

"I know. That's what I keep saying," Eddy said, unable to unravel his jumble of joy and confusion. "You're all wet now."

Eddy helped pull Melanie upright, and they both sat like statues on the side of the bed.

"Aw snap, that's my dad," Melanie said, alerted by a sound on the other side of the house.

Again, Eddy understood and rushed to get his clothes on as Melanie did the same. Melanie beat him getting dressed by a good half a lap around the bed, so she went over to open the escape window, but Eddy, driven by distraught passion, had a different idea.

"What? Not that way," Melanie said emphatically as loudly as she dared, but she saw that it was too late to avert him. Enroute to her door, she hid the towel and the bottle of lubricant with a swing of the comforter and then proceeded out of her room after Eddy. She found Eddy looking around the kitchen, already having discovered that her father had boarded himself up in the master bedroom for a shower. "You're not meeting my dad," Melanie scolded but deserted her sour look as she pushed him with eagerness toward the front steps. Before she pushed him outside, she pulled him back into an embrace and kissed him twice more. "It was a dream vacation," she summarized before nearly hitting his shoulder with the closing swing of the door.

Eddy walked to the street sidewalk and looked back at the house. His face was plastered with the stoic realization that he felt cheaper and of more inconvenience than a plastic pawn of opposing color unable to retreat on Melanie's chess board. Since his legs wanted to collapse and his lungs wanted to leap, he fought away both feelings and started toward home. When he reached the main street, the push of wind hit him along with another realization. His aunt or mom, or both, would be wondering where he was. Responsively, he pulled out his phone, and sure enough, there were two concerned text messages waiting for him.

Chapter Seven

"Eddy!" a girl hollered from behind the young man who had just reached the front steps of the school.

Eddy turned, but before he could say hello, Melanie ran into him, delivering a sparking kiss. The nearby students that missed the collision had no proof of Melanie's rocket kiss but stood gazing nonetheless for the heartbeat that Melanie looked to be gossiping in Eddy's ear. "Despite what anybody says, you won. Can I see you at my place after volleyball practice?"

Melanie's rocket booster ignited Eddy's own shuttle of desires and made him want to spill the feathers that had been tickling his heart all night and all morning. However, his heart pillow was stuffed to its limits and stretched to the point of incapacitation, plus Melanie was too brief. So, off hopped Melanie without an answer into the school, leaving Eddy ruminating a few steps behind.

Scott was waiting with a few of his large teammates, and as soon as Melanie approached to try to kiss him, he asked, "So have you banged that bastard yet?"

Melanie turned to see that he was referencing Eddy, who was ten paces away. "He's a romantic, unlike you. Give us till this weekend."

"I figured he was scared," Scott accused, trying to include his friends in his statement. "You'd better let him know that he's about to miss his chance at your pussy."

"Would you be glad if he did?" Melanie investigated as she linked up to Scott's arm, giving up on her kiss.

Scott ignored her question with a huff and took leave of his friends.

When she posed the question to Scott again with her eyes, she only saw more aggravation, so she gave up on the topic altogether.

As Eddy waited for Melanie to disappear with Scott down the hallway, Rod Dexter, a nosier friend than Charles, interrupted his gaze, asking, "Are you really having sympathy sex with Melanie Westin?"

"Sympathy sex? That's a new phrase," Eddy answered as he turned toward his math class.

"That's what people are saying."

"And I guess it just bugs you enough that you had to ask," Eddy said, stopping to look at Rod's eager face. "It's really a private matter, I hope you understand."

"Hah, private matter," Rod laughed.

"You like that one?" Eddy responded before entering his class to take his seat next to Alexis.

The bell commenced the teacher's instructions for the quarterly quiz, and he started handing the paper assessment out to the rows of students. "When you're done, you have permission to sit and talk quietly in the hallway, or study if you'd prefer."

The students knew the rules of that privilege well and started filling in their answers as soon as the quiz arrived on their desks.

Eddy by far was neither the first nor the last one finished, but he finished at the same time as Alexis and followed her outside of the classroom after delivering his quiz answers to the teacher.

They both quietly sat down together in the hallway like they had been told to do.

"So how was your night?" Alexis asked, breaking the ice.

Thinking she might be fishing for validation to the gossip, Eddy vaguely answered, "It was the best night I've had for as long as I can remember. How was yours?"

"Well, it wasn't that great. I babysat my sister and studied for the quiz."

"How'd you think you did?" Eddy politely asked, looking over at her pleasantly freckled cheek for his answer. Her skin looked whiter than it had previously though still unmistakably Native American.

"Good enough. How's your mom doing?"

"She seems fine," Eddy answered a bit too contritely and thought of his mother's most recent rebuke.

"How about you? How are you doing?"

"I'm fine," Eddy said, feeling uncomfortable with the pressing reminder of his buried thoughts: thoughts of Melanie's kind and comforting lips surfacing to the point that he could almost feel them on his own; thoughts of her eyes and her hands, first at dinner and then on their vacation and how they were devoted, in both cases, still more to Scott, if not devoted to him completely; thoughts of how creep was such a harsh word that she had used to categorize his true affections; thoughts of her kiss and joy that he had enjoyed yet that very morning, affections she had flippantly rent and buried upon entering the school lobby; thoughts evoking feelings, feelings evoking confusion, and confusion wanting an answer to the question: What could possibly be in her best interest now?

Alexis's voice trembled as she said, "I don't know what I would do, or how I'd feel, knowing the next time I saw my dad would be the last time I ever did, and that he wouldn't even hear me say goodbye." Alexis stared at the opposite wall like the flat paint was a puzzle of some deep sort. Upon coming to and finding the flat wall in focus, she heard her thought triggering the mutiny of all of Eddy's thoughts. His thoughts all drained out at once, and when she looked over, she regretted speaking her sentiment.

Eddy tried to blink away what was obvious and struggled to explain, "I hadn't thought about there being a funeral."

"I'm sorry. Do you know when it will be?" Alexis asked, unsure of how to repair her words.

"I don't know," Eddy admitted, trying to repress emotion, but his magmatic thoughts had built up far beyond containment. Thus, he wept bitterly with torturous tears puffing up his eyes and an earthquake tremoring his lungs in waves.

Alexis sat penitently silent and looked guilty for instigating the topic as Eddy's uncharacteristic behavior assembled all the eyes and suppressed all the whispers of his nearby classmates. Eventually, the teacher stepped out into the hallway and called the class back into the room. When Eddy remained put, the teacher could see why and walked over to him.

"Are you okay?"

"I will be," Eddy alluded without much eye contact.

"Take as much time as you need," the teacher allowed and returned to finish teaching the class.

Eddy waited till the class was dismissed. Then dismally, he entered the room and gathered his things. He noticed Alexis was waiting for him by the front of his row, and he acknowledged her with puffy eyes but avoided approaching her to hasten his departure to the office. Once inside the safe space, he asked the secretary to see the counselor. When the counselor finally appeared, Eddy feebly found the words to request his early dismissal and then left the school with the counselor's permission.

Eddy intentionally took his time walking home, but time was all mixed up. He found himself unlocking the door, but he had no memory of passing either the convenience store or Alexis's house.

"You're home early," Kristy said from the couch looking up from her laptop with her glasses resting on her nose. "You okay?"

The question was simple enough for Eddy to answer; the difficulty that tipped his barrel again was his trying to fake it.

Kristy could see the struggle and gladly shoved her workspace aside and moved straight over to hug Eddy before he could escape the foyer.

"Can I miss him?" Eddy asked after crying over Kristy's shoulder uncontrollably for a time.

"If you didn't, people would think you didn't care about him much," Kristy encouraged, choking over her own tears. After Eddy seemed to want to let go, Kristy asked, "Are you hungry? Can I make you something, or go bring something home?" Trying to decipher an answer from her nephew's lost expression, she prompted, "Hmm?"

"No, I'm just going to go read."

"Okay, I'll make some lunch in an hour or so."

Hidden behind his sticker-plastered door with a knot in his stomach, Eddy flopped onto his bed. After a long and blurry analysis of no particular part of his room, he heard his phone buzz. Thinking it might be Alexis trying to apologize anew, he ignored it. But after considering that it could be Melanie asking about his whereabouts, he rolled over and powered up the screen. Neither were true. Another pornographic text alert was all that waited for him. Giving into his moment of weakness, he clicked on the link, but when the images of half-clothed girls appeared in seductive positions, he repulsively chucked his phone at his dresser with clenched teeth, angry for the message even being there. After the phone crashed to the ground, he heard a second tumbling and shattering. After a few more heaves of fuming, he flipped his head over and saw that one of his cherished pictures had been knocked off its stand and off the dresser. Which one had fallen was unclear because of the unforgiving pressure he had been putting on his eyes, but the unintentional consequence quieted his rage to a degree.

Still, like a stubborn ice glacier, he refused to move or melt, that is until the sun that was obnoxiously cheering through the window made him start to sweat. The uncomfortable temperature was what finally convinced him to go inspect the new mess he had made. Then looking around his room, he realized how awfully messy it all was, as if the picture that had fallen had been solely responsible for keeping the many messes from his view. Closing his eyes, he vividly remembered Melanie's room and how it had been, and the comparison embarrassed him. His parents' room and their guest room, on that same scale, were always welcoming and tidy too. Finding inspiration in all three standards, Eddy welcomed the diversion, and he set about his own space, moving, shifting, folding, trashing, and generally arranging things so that the floor eventually reappeared in incremental fashion.

Kristy started noting the strange noises coming from upstairs after the heartbreaking crash. Then when she had heard multiple runs of the vacuum cleaner, her curiosity motivated her off the couch. After climbing the stairs and inconspicuously seeing the cause, she silently retreated to her work. An hour later, Kristy had lunch ready as promised, and Eddy agreed to take a break at Kristy's bidding.

"When's the funeral?" Eddy asked, keeping his eyes cast down to his plate.

"Saturday, from 10am to 5pm," Kristy answered and watched Eddy eat the rest of his lunch in silence.

Eddy went back to cleaning until sweat again made his hair sticky and his clothes wet. Pausing in the midst of his worry-consuming agenda, he sat down on his recrafted bed and heard his phone buzz. It was five o'clock. Having tossed the device on his bed earlier, he slumped over and picked it up. A flip of the phone and a few presses of his thumb showed him that he had a text from Alexis as well as two from Melanie. He opened Melanie's first.

"Where are you? I'm worried," Eddy read and saw that the time stamp correlated to when he would have been called tardy for health class. Then he read, "I'm coming over...if I can figure out where over is." Amused, Eddy texted back his address. Then he pulled up Alexis's text. "Eddy, I got your number from Charles. I feel bad for bringing up your dad the way I did. I hope you don't hate me. Forgive me, please. —Alexis." Eddy wrote back, "I can't forgive a friend for being a friend. Even if she made me cry."

Eddy had a warm smile on his face until he saw himself in his bedroom mirror. Then freaking out like the bathtub was overflowing, he ripped some clean clothes out of his closet and raced to the bathroom. In the rush of changing his shirt, he thought he heard the doorbell ring, but upon pausing, he only heard the fading honks of a goose overhead. Nevertheless, he resumed his hurry for the chance it had rung. Abandoning his dishevelment of hair after an impatient glance and a finger critique, he swung open the bathroom door and nearly put his head through the ceiling when he detected the distinct sound of Melanie's laugh coming from downstairs.

Eddy sobered himself and walked down to see Melanie waiting for him in the living room across from Kristy. "Hi, Mel," Eddy said, addressing both of their glances.

"Hi. You were ignoring my texts."

"Actually, I was cleaning my room."

"He actually was," Kristy corroborated.

"I'd like to go for a walk," Melanie suggested, already on her feet and approaching Eddy.

"I'd like to go with you," Eddy said and waited for Melanie to pass him.

"Good, cause that's what I meant."

Eddy and Melanie hit the sidewalk and started walking like two spontaneous squirrels. Melanie's erratic pattern stemmed from her free state of mind and the fact she had no idea what she was doing, how she was going to accomplish it, or why her heart was strangled with thoughts of Eddy. On the contrary, Eddy moved in response to Melanie, fatigued from the emotion and physical stress he had borne through the entirety of the day while barricaded in his room.

"All I could think about today was how I felt after having sex with you yesterday," Melanie said after taking Eddy's available hand.

"Yeah, me too," Eddy said, forgetting to put any emotion into his response.

Melanie was gleaming at Eddy until she saw that he was intent on not looking at her. This sent a scared look homing after him while her thoughts retaliated, and it took the next few steps without twisting her shoulders or spunkily kicking her feet to command her feet to stop.

Eddy stopped two steps ahead of Melanie and turned around to look at her, but after connecting with her eyes and hinting at his distraction, his look fell.

"Hey," Melanie beckoned.

"Hey, look at me," Melanie insisted, moving around affectionately and shrinking herself to place her eyes in view of Eddy's turned down gaze. "Hey, I'm selfish. Okay?" Melanie said, finally sliding her hands through the hair on either side of Eddy's head to force him to look up at her own tears.

"I didn't want to cry."

Melanie drew him in for a supportive hug. "Hey, I have tissues and two dry shoulders. Come on," Melanie encouraged, knowing there was a school park somewhere around the corner.

Eddy easily kissed Melanie for over an hour before they decided it was time to walk back to the house. When Eddy had stuck his head inside and announced their arrival, he found that his mom was still out. Unconcerned with his discovery, he turned around to find that Melanie had already taken a seat on one of the welcoming porch chairs.

"I realized something," Melanie said, asking Eddy to sit down by holding out her open hand.

"What'd you realize?" Eddy asked, trusting Melanie with his fingers.

Melanie looked at Eddy and instantly had second thoughts about her statement, but feeling on the spot to speak, she said, "You're a smart guy."

"That's better than being a wise-guy. Right?" Eddy countered, sensing that Melanie had hidden her honesty.

Melanie acknowledged his pun with her pleasant lips, knowing she had given away too much of what she was thinking in her pause.

Screeching, the garage door shuddered to life and both students looked as Cynthia pulled into the driveway. After waving and parking, Cynthia emerged from the garage sideways with a grocery bag in both hands and greeted, "Hi, Melanie! It's good to see you again. Are you staying for dinner?"

"No, I'm afraid not. This little rascal here hasn't invited me," Melanie replied, looking briefly at Eddy, but she continued in the same breath before Eddy had a chance to fix his alleged impoliteness, "Actually, Mrs. Kraft, my dad expects me home, but I wanted to ask you something before I go."

"Sure," Cynthia responded, delaying her entrance to the house.

"I understand there's a funeral this Saturday, and I want to know if I'd be intruding by accompanying your son, even though I haven't asked him yet. Is that okay?"

Cynthia's lips moved like they meant to speak, but they closed without doing so. Shifting her groceries, she looked at Eddy, who was lost in his own blank stare, and finding no objection, she responded, "I'll leave that up to you two, but I'll be sure to leave you a seat in our car."

When Cynthia had disappeared through the doorway, Melanie looked back at Eddy's thinking face like a submissive puppy, looking equally for an apology and permission. "May I...be your friend this weekend?"

"What about Scott? People will see you with me," Eddy warned.

"I don't want Scott to stop me from supporting my friend," Melanie assured. "So?"

"Thank you. That'd mean more to me than everything you've given me," Eddy said with appreciation fastened to his cheeks, appreciation that could have easily been read as a scowl had his words not been so tender.

"I haven't given you much. I can do better."

"May I walk you home?" Eddy asked, feeling the furnace of his heart kick on to full heat.

"If you say *hi* to my dad when we get there," Melanie conditioned before she stood up to accept Eddy's offer.

Eddy's eyes displayed his churning brain, and his slow interpretation of Melanie's stipulation seeped onto the rest of his boyish face like a cheerful color of paint bleeding onto a canvass. When Melanie saw that Eddy understood, she happily emphasized her inference with a look and stood up on her tingling toes. Together, both students stepped inside to inform Cynthia and Kristy of their destination before hitting the sidewalk again, this time in the other direction.

--- *Great Gravitations: Journal page thirty-seven written that peaceful evening from my orderly bedroom.*

I can't fully tell you how therapeutic it is to kiss a girl when you're feeling sad. Kissing Melanie in the park made me feel like I was able to release my emotions and say things I was scared to admit about my dad, all without stuttering through the details or drenching her soft shoulders. It was as if, when my heart would deliver a reason to cry, she would intercept it with a kiss and then the same tear that I was about to shed would appear on her cheek. And if I would try to take the tear back, she wouldn't let go of it. I'll admit, when I saw her house, I got nervous. On her front porch, I didn't catch whether she had said that her dad wasn't home or wasn't coming out, but either way she apologized with another kiss. Feelings are strange. As much as I want to say that having sex with Melanie was in her best interest the day before, I can't now because it wasn't. Oh how I want to shake Scott and say, "Man, are you crazy! You want your girlfriend to be *banged*, so you can sleep around for your own fun? She needs to be hugged and kissed and needs you to care about her and her dad. And she needs it so much that she's giving me, some boy that she made a whimsical bet on, the chance to do it for you." Come on, Scott!

Chapter Eight

--- Great Gravitations: Journal page fifty-three, written after finishing that first, emotional, bipolar, and dad-less week of school while sitting in the bleachers and watching a Friday night game of volleyball spikes, rebounds, and sets over a girl's regulation height net.

I must say that I thought I knew how pretty Melanie was, but every time I see her in the hall or look at her in class, I see something about her that makes her prettier still. Like how she'll kiss Scott's shoulder before she lets go of his arm, or how she'll immediately look to see if Scott is laughing at something the teacher said that she thought was funny. It doesn't seem to matter, I came down with another case of puffy-red-eyes after health class, and I still can't differentiate whether it's triggered by my dad or because of Melanie giving her love and attention to Scott...probably both.

--- The time neared a quarter past 9:00am the next morning inside a greasy maintenance bay at Melanie's dad's workplace.

"Dad, we have to go!" Melanie emphasized while trying to keep her dad in a good mood.

"You're the one that wanted to go shopping for a black dress," Frank Westin refuted gruffly while searching for the right tool on his work bench.

"I did, and I've been dressed for twenty minutes now. But wouldn't this be a good place to stop working?" Melanie suggested, trying to sound positive again to manage her father's mood.

"I'm almost done," Frank said, rolling back under his vehicle that had coughed and jolted into the bay of his employer's mechanic shop. The underside of the car had already consumed every bit of time that his daughter had asked to be early at her new boyfriend's house, and after wrenching a bit more on something around the front axle, Frank said, "There."

"Dad, you're making the car leak instead of taking me to Eddy's," Melanie observed, letting a hint of complaint creep into her words.

"Yeah, yeah," Frank said in his unhindered rough voice, and he started wiping his hands. "Do you want to know why I made the car start leaking, or why I think the car lurched to a stop three times on the way back from the store when I put it in gear? I don't think we would have made it to that boy's house at all," Frank continued, lowering his volume when he saw the resigned desperation on his daughter's face. This was his equivalent to softening the tone of his rock-filled vocal cords. "At least being here at the garage, Johnny might let me borrow his ride for an hour."

Melanie sprang so thankfully with joy that her dad unconsciously reflected her expression back at her as he unzipped his oversized coveralls. His coveralls were oversized due to the size of his upper body, specifically the breadth of his shoulders, and this special-order mechanic's garment, being extremely baggy on his lower half, comically made Frank look like he wore poorly designed bell-bottoms. Melanie got her height from him and a few of her other attractive features, such as her eye color and the shape of her nose. Anyone could clearly see that she was Frank's daughter, and though Frank was undeniably Melanie's father, he had never married, for, despite his physique and good enough looks, he had no compassion, only matter-of-factness.

"Johnny, she's down again. Do you have any place to be for an hour?" Frank called across the garage.

"No, sir! Don't put a dent in her!" the muffled reply came from his boss.

--- *After cruising across town in Johnny's 1965 baby-blue convertible, Frank and Melanie were nearing Eddy's house.*

"Would you come inside to just meet him and his mom, please?" Melanie asked as nicely as she could after having petitioned her father once already while leaving Johnny's garage.

Frank had already answered, and a gruff look returned to his face as he pulled to a stop in front of the requested address. "I have a lot to do, honey."

"Two seconds. He's coming out to meet you now. See?" Melanie pointed, stalling her egress to prevent her dad from pulling away.

Eddy had appeared at the front door and waved, but misinterpreted Melanie's signal as she needed to first finish with her dad, so he waited to see where he was.

Melanie realized what might have happened and stepped out of the car, calling, "Come here, silly." Running her fingers through her free-spirited hair, she turned around with excitement but saw her dad's final sentiment as clearly as her reflection in the chrome side-mirror. "Hey, thank you so much, Dad. You can go," she switched impulsively, afraid of Eddy getting a bad impression. At his cue of understanding, she turned around and wrapped her arms around Eddy's neck like a bow on a package. As if waiting to be opened, she left her arms in place for as long as she felt the snugness on her back. Meanwhile her dad drove off.

"Your dress is very pretty on you," Eddy complimented, having no idea that she had tried on five different ones at the store earlier that morning.

"It's new," Melanie said with her chin still on Eddy's shoulder. "My dad bought it for me today."

Eddy felt as special as a rose bush decorated with enviable flowers.

"I even had to bite the tags off so I could wear it here."

Eddy hardly said anything for the rest of the day, and Melanie kept her distance, only trying to hold his hand on the car rides and when they were about to approach the open casket. But even then, Melanie stepped back to let his mother comfort him as he cried. Melanie mostly felt lost in the sea of strange faces, at least a thousand of them.

--- *Thirty-six hours after the funeral, with his Monday morning backpack on and his superhero T-shirt showing off his elbows, Eddy walked to school at an okay pace.*

"I finally timed it correctly," Eddy said as he watched Alexis pull her front door closed.

"You've been trying?" Alexis asked cynically, seeing that Eddy had stopped at the end of her driveway under the greedy overhangs of her oak tree.

"You must have slept in."

"You must have left early," Alexis replied, comfortably competing with Eddy's wit.

"I saw you on Saturday," Eddy said appreciatively.

"I...I didn't know what to say, so I just went like I guess so many others did. You didn't look like you wanted to talk. Besides, Melanie was always beside you," Alexis said, her countenance shifting to show her discomfort.

"I'm glad you came. It all was a blur. It felt like half of the school showed up," Eddy said, sensing Alexis's discomfort as they progressed out of their neighborhood. "I hardly recognized people. But I recognized a few friendly faces, one of them being yours."

"So, do you think Scott will care that Melanie is acting like she likes you?" Alexis asked, letting her question hang like a broken fingernail for Eddy to consider.

"She said she didn't care what Scott thought and didn't want Scott choosing how she supported her friend," Eddy honestly responded, feeling the tender pang of his conscience poke his chest.

"You guys are more than friends," Alexis said, releasing an unbelieving laugh.

"Why do you say that?" Eddy asked, trying to sound inquisitive but feeling guilty.

"Because it takes more than basic friendship to make this feel comfortable," Alexis said, slipping her hand into Eddy's to make her point. Straightway releasing his hand out of respect, Alexis waited for Eddy to react.

Eddy wrenched his mouth closed to prevent his initial reaction from zapping Alexis for her forwardness. Then after he settled the lion growling in his heart, he admitted with a tempered voice, "You got me right, but I don't know about Melanie yet."

Alexis looked like she had in the hallway at school, ashamed for having unlocked the topic, and she diverted her eyes to the traffic on the street.

Noticing Alexis's distance, Eddy continued, "When Melanie's around me, she acts like more than a friend, but I lose that extra part of her when she's around Scott. There's something he has that I don't." Eddy shook his head at himself. "But I do know she's not acting when she's around me, and I do know how she makes me feel," Eddy finished, keeping his eyes on the crosswalk and away from Alexis.

Daringly, Alexis looked at Eddy and asked, "How do I make you feel?"

"Playful, witty, bold," Eddy responded straightway enough to be convincing.

"No, how do I make *you* feel?" Alexis repeated with emphasis.

"You make me feel playful, witty, and bold. I'm glad we're in class together," Eddy clarified as they passed the convenience store.

After giving Eddy plenty of time to return the question, she showed her buried frustration. "Are you even going to ask?"

"Ask you what?" Eddy investigated, still trapped in the maze of his earlier thoughts.

"How I feel about you," Alexis answered harshly and started walking ahead with fitful and rapid strides.

"Alexis, that's not fair," Eddy objected, and to show how stubborn he was himself, he hopped to keep pace with her.

"I want to know," he insisted as the school approached faster than usual.

Having scowled along with tunnel vision, Alexis stopped suddenly at the bottom of the school steps and realized that Eddy had kept up with her unfair pace the entire way. So there on the first step like a tottering hot kettle, she spilled, "No guy has ever talked to me like you do. I woke up every morning this week thinking about math. And not because I like math, but only because I get to sit next to you. And then I go to your father's funeral because you've called me your friend, and Melanie is there smothering you which makes me feel like your second-rate friend." Alexis's chest rose and fell before she looked away.

Eddy took a deep breath of his own and dropped down onto one knee. Looking up, he took Alexis's hand away from her side, and said "This is...this is not me asking you out. This is me asking you: How do I fix this?" Eddy could see his mom's words of warning clearly on Alexis's face.

"Kiss me," Alexis said from her heart, dreading the reaction she anticipated.

"I can't right now, Alexis. I'm sorry. But I can walk you to class," Eddy offered, flustering his kind offer like a butcher on his first day of the job.

"I can walk myself," Alexis emotionally concluded and walked herself directly to her math-class seat and sat down in a terrible mood. After Eddy settled next to her, she put her bag down on the floor and put her head down on her arm.

--- *Great Gravitations: Journal page seventy-two, written outside of the gymnasium, using the ticket office wall for support as I listened to the squeaks and pounds of Melanie's volleyball practice.*

I felt horrible for my entire first-hour class and avoided making any attempt to talk to Alexis afterward. The rest of the day was different though. The turnaround started with a look and a touch from Melanie as I passed her in the hallway after my second-hour class. She was walking with one of her friends and reached out without slowing her pace any. Her passing fingers caught the side of my hand like a leafy branch catching the cuff of a hiker's shirtsleeve, and she hooked it like she meant to interrupt the time of a grandfather clock by stalling the pendulum. That's my English assignment by the way, to come up with similes to share with the class. Then in health class, my overinflated mind nearly popped. Scott walked in and sat down by a friend. Then as the bell was calling her tardy, Melanie came in and chose a much different seat to the befuddlement of everyone.

--- *Two class periods earlier, the moment was monstrous after all eyes turned with rapid-fire to analyze Melanie's peculiar choice of seating.*

"Uh, hello?!" Scott called, breaking up the rush of murmuring comments.

Eddy could see courage stiffening Melanie's jaw and saw her eyes looking for permission to stay seated across from him.

"Hello, Melanie? Are you blind or deaf?"

"You can't hear her thinking?" Eddy questioned with positivity to divert Scott's offensive and simultaneously acknowledge Melanie's looking cry for help.

A few students chuckled.

"Shut up, dweeb."

"Okay," Eddy said and reclined in his seat, unable to think of a more defensive word.

"Mel, why aren't you sitting over here? I saved you your seat," Scott said, changing his offended approach.

"I have changed opinions, so deal with it," Melanie said, standing her ground.

Steven Kloomsfield, dressed in his gray blazer and maroon T-shirt, timely walked into the room. With one look, he noticed but ignored the odd fact that Melanie was not leaning on Scott.

"Umm...Mr. Kloomsfield? I'd like to make an observation in regard to where people have elected to sit today," Scott said with irritation, his eyebrows simmering on his face, his face swelling on his neck, and his neck displacing his tightened shoulders.

"Go ahead," Steven said, bracing for the foolishness that he knew was about to scold his ears.

"I think that since Eddy is banging my girlfriend, and that they're not doing it behind my back either, they should both be sitting over here at this table, since that is pretty much exactly what this table's sex position is about."

Students responsively laughed at the grittiness of Scott's unintentional pun which perplexed Scott a bit. Then when Mr. Kloomsfield was about to enact crowd control to level the bump in the road, Melanie beat him to his hammer and defended herself with a piece of her mind, scolding, "Why don't you take a hint, Scott. Maybe you should ask me privately why I'm choosing to sit over here."

"And why can't you just say thank you for me allowing you to embark off on your little sex bet with Eddy. Hurray. Your virgin sex buddy isn't a virgin anymore. You say thank you, and I'll say you're welcome," Scott argued, trying to pull tempered reason out of his obvious frustration.

"That sounds a lot more like having a sexual relationship based on mutual terms, Scott," Melanie defended, and reclining in her chair, she apologized to the teacher by lending him her attention with her arms folded.

"I hope you're not falling for this orphaned creep," Scott retaliated, unwilling to give up the last word.

Melanie flashed her eyes to Eddy and would rather have read an entire French dictionary than his blank stare in the interval of time their instructor stood stupefied from Scott's thoughtless outburst. Jealously wanting an hour alone with Eddy in that moment, she impulsively fired back, "It turns out Frankenstein knows how to please me better than you, Captain."

Melanie knew her innuendo struck gold when the corners of Eddy's mouth curled upward, and because Steven Kloomsfield caught all of Scott Ardan's inappropriate assault and understood none of Melanie's cryptic tongue, he sent Scott into the hallway for the rest of the period.

--- *Great Gravitations: The end of journal page seventy-two and the start of page seventy-three. (The other half of my entry that I had written outside of Melanie's volleyball practice, outside because Scott Ardan was sitting on the first row of the bleachers inside.)*

I guess if that's all my purpose is, I can live with that, and I guess too that means I finally have my answer to what's in Melanie's best interest. I mean, I hope I never have to get hit by a two-by-four like Scott did to reignite my passion for someone. And I'm glad I didn't blow off Alexis for sake of my fanciful notion that somehow my friend-with-benefits relationship was going to somehow morph into true companionship. It hurts a little, maybe, but not more than Alexis seemed to be hurt this morning. I guess I'm Frankenstein, and Scott is Captain. Maybe I'll find another box of Mike & Kie Fruits, or maybe Alexis will start talking to me again. Who knows? I'm still glad Melanie started schooling Scott a bit on what she wants, and I hope she shows him the inferiority of his choice term for sex. Like I've written already, what sane girl wants to be banged?

Chapter Nine

"Hey, Mel, are you free after practice?" Scott asked after school, finding Melanie at her locker. He then politely offered to carry her volleyball gear when she turned around and stared at him flatly. Scott had tried to apologize after health class but had only gotten a deserving sour expression from Melanie for his public showdown. Deservingly, he had stewed over the shunning for his entire next two class periods, but his stewing was what led him into productively planning a date with Melanie, a date for after her volleyball practice. Scott's unusual presence in the bleachers during practice was the reason why Eddy had wisely decided it best not to journal his thoughts of the day inside the gymnasium.

"Me? Free?" Melanie asked. "Why, whatever had you in mind to do after school with me?"

Scott could almost see the sarcasm dripping from Melanie's grammar. "Somehow try to show you that I'm not an imbecile," Scott reasoned, maintaining a closed posture while the inferred apology resonated on Melanie's face. "Maybe we could walk to the park, or the mall. And you know I know the best ice cream shop in town. We could stop there first if you'd like," Scott suggested without assuming her answer for once.

"Take me mall walking and ice cream shopping," Melanie said, smiling involuntarily at Scott's expression.

"In that order?"

"Make a plan, Captain," Melanie ordered indifferently. She could tell the name still irritated him, and she let him know it with her still skeptical eyes.

"Great! And hey, I'm sorry for...for embarrassing you during health class."

"He says *I'm sorry*!" Melanie celebrated, and throwing her arms up in victory, she spun around and jumped onto his neck.

Scott easily caught Melanie's weight, and she hung on him and kissed him to prolong her hanging.

"You are sexy," Scott complimented.

"Yeah?"

"Totally."

"Can you love me slowly like Teddy Eddy did?" Melanie requested.

"Totally!"

"Oh, pandemonium! I'm excited about our mall walking now," Melanie said, running away and then walking back for a kiss. "I mean, pressure's on," Melanie challenged, recomposing flippantly, and she eyed Scott up and down with a judging act before walking away again.

"Gobstoppers! She's either crazy, or I'm crazy about her," Scott said to himself before he started following her to the gymnasium to watch her team practice.

--- The young couple cut short their mall-walking plans with an unplanned stop at Melanie's vacant house, and once inside, they very soon found themselves interrupting the order of Melanie's bedroom.

"Okay, okay, I know you're excited. Slow down," Melanie suppressed as she tried to keep up with Scott kissing her.

Scott had his shirt off already and had his hands all over Melanie. "Damn, you're attractive," Scott said when his mouth was leaping from one part to his next target.

"What an unattractive thing to say to a girl you like," Melanie complained, letting her pants and underwear come off.

"You're funny," Scott said, missing Melanie's displeasure.

"No, Scott. Please don't bite me. No, no, no! No penis yet," Melanie discouraged, from her position on her bed.

"What? That's what sex is. The faster I move, the faster you come," Scott said, pausing his advance.

"The faster you...where did you learn that fallacy?" Melanie complained.

"From the internet; where else?"

"Okay, how about this. I'll take care of you. Come. Lie down, stud," Melanie invited rashly to take control, tapping the bed and trying to slow down her words. "And you can take care of me. You can take care of me, can't you?" Melanie asked, playing to Scott's ego.

"Okay."

"No penis," Melanie reminded.

"Whatever. Now you've got the touch!" Scott commented.

"Don't you want me to enjoy this too?" Melanie asked when Scott had passively settled his head on his hands.

"Why'd you stop?"

"Because you haven't started," Melanie protested with a scoffing laugh.

Scott huffed and started massaging Melanie where she had requested.

Melanie then started playing again, trying to get in the mood as Scott's romancing sputtered like a vapor-locked motor. Grudgingly abandoning her hope, she turned and started kissing which only encouraged Scott back onto his bobsled course.

"Scott, goodness. Vocabulary...slow down. I'm not a sex doll!"

"Come on, baby. I want to love on you."

"Scott! Seriously, no penis. Stop, please! That doesn't even feel good!"

"Well...aren't you just being difficult. Hold still."

"Scott, that's not sexy, and it hurts."

"It'll be all over in a minute."

"Please stop! You're talking like a—" Melanie strained as forcefully as she could, but midsentence there was thunderous commotion at her door, and Scott was pulled and thrown on the floor all at once like her choking appeal had been a powerful punch.

"Get your clothes on, kid!" Frank Westin commanded, putting himself in position to pound punishment into the boy if he disobeyed.

"Dad, I'm sorry. It just got out of hand. I invited him in here," Melanie explained with horror as she watched her boyfriend gracelessly fall over himself next to her dresser. She was just as scared of her father's wrath as the boy scrambling to get his clothes on.

On cue, Frank's dominating voice flew like a whip, "Melanie, I don't care what boyfriends you give your body to, but no boy on this planet is too dumb to not understand the words please and stop. Now get out! The next time I see you on my property, you'll have buckshot in your behind," Frank said, pushing the boy down the hallway after he had waited patiently enough for the boy to find his shoes. "And don't come back!" Frank

threatened as he nearly pushed the boy out the front door and
down the cement riser. Watching the boy run and check over
his shoulder twice, Frank waited again. When the boy finally
disappeared down the sidewalk, Frank locked the front door and
returned to check on his daughter.

Embarrassed to the point of shaking, Melanie was already fully
clothed and was pushing the wrinkles out of her bed when her
dad stepped inside her door with a commanding huff of
disapproval.

"Daddy?" Melanie sobbed after she had spun around to face
his presence.

"Mel," Frank replied with a condescending disappointment
meant to trump any manipulative remark that could have been
forming in Melanie's head.

"Daddy?" Melanie repeated, shivering harder and covering
herself with her arms. "I've had sex with him before. He's—I
thought."

"Mel, you over-estimate the thickness of these walls," Frank
scolded when his daughter's confession started falling apart.
"I'm not happy, but I want to clarify something I said after I tore
that thug away from holding you down," Frank continued, his
words staggering because of their significance.

Melanie took an asking step toward the protection of her
father, and when she saw his invitation open, she moved the rest
of the way into his embrace.

"Mel."

"Yes?" Melanie asked, receiving the entirety of her father's hug
while having forgotten to uncross her arms.

"Mel. I do care who my daughter gives herself to. In fact, I'd
like the chance...I know I've been difficult, but...I would
like...would like you to give me the chance to know your
friends...your boyfriends."

"I've been trying with that one, Daddy," Melanie admitted as
she listened to her father's rhythmic heartbeat.

"That one...that boy will not set foot in this house again,
unless—no. That one's done, unless you want trouble. And I
mean he-can-give-his-apology-from-the-sidewalk done. Do you
understand?"

"That makes it easier," Melanie said, loving her father's authority and embrace.

"I love you, Mel."

"Daddy?"

"Yes, Mel?"

"Another boy has been much gentler with me. Would you meet him?" Melanie asked and listened to her father take an intimidating breath.

"Was it that boy? That funeral you went to?"

"Yes, Daddy," Melanie confirmed. "Eddy Kraft. I've had sex with him too, but he was different."

"Well, aren't we confessing everything today."

"He wanted to meet you, Daddy. You wouldn't have to protect me from him," Melanie contended, letting peace influence her expression when her father refrained from scolding her.

"I can't always be there to protect you, Mel."

Melanie understood and snuggled her cheek further into her father's chest. When Frank finally released his thick arms from behind Melanie, he stepped back and looked at his daughter like a skilled detective. Seeing her hair out of place and tangled, he asked, "Do you remember what I used to do when you were knee high with that beautiful hair of yours?"

"Yeah," Melanie replied and hoped her father would offer to comb and braid her hair.

"I used to comb and put your hair in pig tails."

"Until I was eight, and I realized how awful you were at it," Melanie said, adding her perspective of his endearing activity.

"Well, I won't claim I was good at braiding, but I think I always did a fair job brushing it beforehand."

"Would you now?" Melanie requested with hesitant eagerness and stepped toward her makeup desk.

"How hard would it be for you to cook a dinner for this Eddy and me one of these nights?" Frank asked his daughter after he started carefully brushing her hair like it was the finest of silks. Frank took his answer from the notable sign of color in the mirror.

--- *Great Gravitations: Journal page seventy-seven, written in the peace and cool of the morning, long before anyone else was awake for breakfast.*

Melanie called me last evening, and we had a five-hour phone conversation. Her voice was definitely different, and she was hinting all around us planning our next date. So, I had to stop her and ask, "What gives?" I don't know how many words she fit into that sentence, but her message was clear enough. Her dad had forced her to break up with Scott. I asked her what happened, and she said that she couldn't tell me unless I was there...that it was something too scary to bring up without me being there to put my arms around her. I wasn't about to complain because that's very much what I wanted to do anyway. I now have my favorite spot in my room to talk to Mel. And hurray! My room has more than one option now that I'm in competition with her spot free space.

I couldn't sleep last night because of Mel and our hours of talking, so I texted her. It's something you must normally do with that special someone, I guess, because Mel texted me back and said, "Honest to goodness," she was about to text me. She said that she couldn't sleep because she couldn't stop thinking about me picking her up from her house tomorrow. I still can't sleep which is why I'm still awake to write this.

--- *After a restless and hazy last hour of sleep, after a rushed breakfast, and after arriving at Melanie's porch steps, Eddy found Melanie waiting and ready behind her front door.*

"Is your dad home?" Eddy asked as he watched Melanie lock herself out of the house.

"No, he works early," Melanie said, liking Eddy's assumed intention. "Well, he works late too. He's just always working."

"Would you respect him if he didn't?" Eddy asked, waiting for Melanie to make one of her hands available.

Seeing Eddy's eyes floating around after her fingers, Melanie emptied her closest hand. "I'll give you one of these for safe keeping if you give me a backpack-less hug," she propositioned, wiggling her fingers slightly in front of Eddy's face.

"That sounds like a win-win if you ask me," Eddy said, dropping his backpack to the ground.

Melanie could envelope Eddy's neck with the inside of her elbows because he was nowhere as broad as Scott and at least a full-inch shorter. Nevertheless, Eddy was the right height to kiss, that is if Melanie wore two-inch heels which is what she had mindfully chosen to wear.

Eddy pulled back from their enjoyable hug and saw Melanie's face dressed in hope. "You are stunning this morning. Radiant like I've never seen you before," Eddy said, trying to hold onto her affectionate pleasure. Eddy gazed, his eyes floating between her brown eyes and naturally shaded lips.

Melanie wanted Eddy to initiate something before she went to high school for the first time without Scott Ardan as her boyfriend. Thus, she had put her lips on a leash, but her eagerness escaped through other parts of her face.

Eddy then finally stopped looking at her nervous lips and slowly moved to kiss them.

"Okay, okay," Melanie said rapturously, needing to breathe. "We're going to be playing hooky if we don't go now."

High on Melanie's gift, Eddy scooped up his backpack and helped Melanie slide hers over her shoulders. Once loaded, with a left hand in a right hand, they set out together like it was their first day of school.

"I have a big question for you."

"Okay, I'm nervous," Eddy said, looking at Melanie.

"Don't be. Okay, be," Melanie said. "I realized something, and I decided something, and I didn't take my birth control this morning. And I don't plan to...continue to. Is that okay with you?" Melanie asked, over-emphasizing her question.

Eddy felt in the dark on how he had any say in that matter, and Melanie took Eddy's confused look as a demand for an explanation.

"Scott wanted me to be on birth control so we could have sex whenever we wanted. I was okay with it because he wanted it, but I really didn't want to, and I want to have kids someday without having any complications like my aunt did after she used birth-control pills for so long," Melanie elucidated but thought her explanation was lacking. "It doesn't mean we can't have sex," Melanie spouted out of last resort but looked away disappointed with her words like she had intended to stick to another principle, but her philosophical mortar had yet to dry.

Eddy was drowning in what was happening, but he saw he needed to say something. "Mel, yes. Nothing drives me wilder than the thought of you wanting to have a baby. And I don't know why. Maybe because it means you want to have sex the way it was meant to be had, but it's your body," Eddy said, thinking he was calming her down. Instead, she seemed more nervous.

"Then, what if I said that...well, would you still want me if I didn't have sex with you till you...till you wed me...till we were married?"

"That sounds a lot more like abstinence," Eddy tried joking, but he still saw some hesitation in Melanie's eyes. "And you'd make me so happy if you said that," Eddy concluded, acknowledging what he valued with an uncontainable expression.

"Really? Or are you just saying that?"

Eddy was still unaware of the needles that Melanie was standing on and of what to say to satisfy her, but he wanted to support her more than ever. So, looking around and swaying desperately for inspiration, he grabbed at a simple thought that came to him. "Okay, let's try an experiment. Come sit over here with me. Sit as close as you can to me, and let's see what happens," Eddy instructed on the fly.

They moved over and plopped down next to each other on a low, brick, border wall. "Now all you have to do is to tell me when you think we're close enough. Are we close enough?" Eddy asked a bit too eagerly before Melanie had settled.

"No," Melanie said, playing along and waiting for his punch line.

"Do you think we could be closer and still be comfortable?"

"Yes," Melanie agreed and slid her backpack off.

Eddy did the same, and they scooted closer together, wrapping their arms around each other. "Are you comfortable?"

"Very."

"Can you get closer and still be comfortable?" Eddy asked one more time.

"Nope," Melanie answered, flashing her interested face at Eddy.

"Then, this is how close we will stay, no closer until you're comfortable with getting closer. And I hope you'll offer me the same comfortable option," Eddy explained, and Melanie leaned her head on Eddy's shoulder.

"Is that comfortable?" Melanie asked.

"Very."

"Thank you, Eddy. I hope you don't think I'm just some girl that's helpless without a guy."

"Don't worry, Mel. I hope you don't think I'm some boy that's just trying to have sex with a girl," Eddy expressed equally, letting his cheek press on Melanie's bed of hair.

"Don't worry, Ed."

"Wait, I thought Ed was blah!" Eddy objected.

"I like options," Melanie confessed, kissing Eddy's hand that hugged her shoulder.

--- *Great Gravitations: Journal page seventy-eight, written after my first-period math class started.*

Time disappears when you're with someone that's being affectionate to you. It's like you're each given an hour to spend, but your hour becomes two hours when you're apart and becomes a half hour when you're together. The walk to school only took ten minutes, and maybe if we had twenty, it wouldn't have felt like five.

--- *After the ten-minute walk to school, Ed and Mel crossed onto the school property to find Scott standing in plain view, waiting at the top of the school steps.*

Melanie told Eddy how nervous she was about this encounter by the heaviness and fervor in her hand. So, he veered their course to circumvent the roadblock that Scott had set up, but the roadblock veered just as well.

"So, what part of *my girlfriend* don't you understand, Eddy?" Scott instigated, moving to get the upper hand.

"I'm not your girlfriend anymore after yesterday," Melanie said, reattaching herself to the jittery rollercoaster of yesterday's emotions. "My dad forbids it and says the only thing you have left to do with me is to apologize. And you're in a lot deeper hole with him than you think, so you can drop the label, please."

"I thought we had a good thing going. I admitted I was a jerk, and I—"

"You couldn't listen, Scott," Melanie said, getting more flustered. "And it doesn't matter now or how red in the face you get. You lost me, Scott. Go find someone else like you did last week," Melanie charged, sending her message clearly.

"I will. But you'll regret this."

"Regret what, Scott? That my dad finally caught us and threw you out of the house because you thought it was okay to pin my throat to the bed?" Melanie theorized like a wielded switchblade. "That actually sounds quite fatherly of him," Melanie added, visually including Eddy in her response because Scott's twitching facial muscles were becoming difficult to watch. "Come on, Scott," Melanie then emotionally reversed, beseeching Scott as he started storming off.

Eddy restrained Melanie as she started to pursue her past boyfriend. "Mel," Eddy said as their two arms tugged at each other. "Hey Mel," Eddy said again, waiting for her attention after she had spun distraughtly around. Melanie looked like she was getting ready to shove Eddy down the school steps with her helpless hands that were fisting his shirt. "I'm so proud of you, Mel...hurray, woohoo!" Eddy whispered over her ear after her forehead had slowly collided with his shoulder.

"I'm glad I have you Eddy. Day one?" Melanie asked, loosened a bit from her stiffness by Eddy's warm words.

"You mean day eleven," Eddy corrected. "You changed the entire course of my life it would seem eleven days ago," Eddy argued.

"Day one. I'm ashamed of how I've used you until this morning."

Eddy's thoughts stopped till he realized that Melanie was standing out in public chest to chest with him. "Does love begin at day one?" Eddy asked. "If it does, then I'm on day four. Because I fell in love with a caring girl in a pretty black dress that bit the tags off of it just so she could look nice and be close to me when she knew I'd be needing somebody."

"You're a dream, Ed," Melanie said, brightening up and touching his lips. "And you officially just made me late for class," Melanie charged as the school bell indicated they would both be tardy.

"What's this about *me* making *you* late?" Eddy objected, scurrying through the school doors behind his girlfriend.

--- *Great Gravitations: Journal page seventy-nine to eighty, written instead of doing the teacher's handout of math problems.*

I can see how parents could accuse girlfriends of damaging your future. Not that I would ever agree with them publicly, but I can see how they'd make their case about it. I have not understood one iota of what the teacher has taught in math today, but maybe that's a good thing. Not all lessons in life need to come from a textbook, right? How about spending time recounting where you fell in love and spending time studying the memories of the person you've fallen in love with? I sure hope Mel picks me for her study group after school. No seriously. We have almost all the same classes. I know I can make this work for us. We can just study at the library or something.

At least Alexis is still ignoring me so my daydreams can be of all things Mel, of things like how I'm blown away by all the implications of Mel wanting to wait for sex. Does she mean that she hopes I'll propose? Does she mean she'll change her table in health class to abstinence? Does she mean waiting to have sex till after she says *Yes* or till after I say *I do*? Plus, where is my standard in all of this? Has it changed too with this change of climate? I'll be completely honest: part of me still feels like I'm not as attractive as Scott is to her, but then again maybe she has realized like my dad told me that healthy relationships aren't all about looks and body shape. Anyway, all trifling worries aside, I'm glad that she's setting us up for the long run instead of the myopic short game.

Chapter Ten

The hallways were scattered with students after first period, so finding Melanie after class was relatively easy for Eddy. In the middle of the flow of students, Eddy caught Melanie, who had walked right up and into his arms.

"What's wrong?" Eddy asked, thinking Melanie would be more enthusiastic.

"Amy and Gabby won't talk to me," Melanie said calmly, liking how Eddy let her nuzzle his shoulder like her father did.

"Can I assume it's because of Scott?" Eddy dug, sliding his arms underneath Melanie's backpack.

"I could go into all the details, but basically they accused me of making Scott freak out," Melanie explained, tilting her chin up to show her appreciation of Eddy's hug.

"Do I have to make a snide remark about their pathetic loyalty, or can we agree that they're being completely ridiculous?"

"Completely ridiculous. Who's giving you all these right words?" Melanie asked, oblivious to the swirl of students around them.

"My mother."

Melanie laughed and coached herself, "Okay. One more hour."

"Meet you back here?" Eddy inquired, letting Melanie's left arm slide out of his hand.

"How about one hallway over?"

"Perfect!" Eddy confirmed before bolting for his next classroom to recover from their shrinkage of time.

--- *After entertaining thoughts, daydreaming, and responsively doodling, Eddy filtered back into the hallway.*

The hour came and went along with another two-minute embrace. Then Melanie was on first lunch. Eddy had to wait for second, and there was about a ten-minute overlap at the beginning as well as at the end of second lunch where both students promised to come looking for each other in the cafeteria.

"Did you hear about Scott?" Charles asked Eddy as they brought up the rear of the unusually lengthy lunch line.

"No. Tell me please," Eddy said, allocating more of his attention to his friend, distracted and disproportionate as it was.

"Apparently, he flipped over his desk first hour. Well, he didn't flip over it, but...like...he pushed his desk over and got sent to the office. I heard he's back in class now," Charles said as he finished off his tray with the last basket of potato-fries.

"Wow," Eddy said, unsure of how to respond as he moved up to hand his payment to the usual lady at the checkout station.

Charles did the same behind him, and they both stepped into the cafeteria. "Are you sitting with that girl today?" Charles asked, curious of how his friend would handle his relations considering his new schoolwide status of being Melanie Westin's boyfriend.

"That girl sitting all alone right there?"

"Yeah."

"I don't know. Should I? I need some advice," Eddy asked without indicating which direction he intended to take.

"Dude, that's your call. Ask me after I mess up my first relationship, and maybe I'd have an answer for you," Charles puffed, still watching Eddy to see which way he would go.

"I'll catch up with you later, Charles," Eddy said and set out for Alexis's table. He walked around behind Alexis and sat down two stools away from her without saying anything. He knew he caught Alexis's attention and forced himself, like a British soldier, not to smile or look her way.

"What are you doing?" Alexis asked with offense.

"Oh. Hi, Alexis," Eddy said and returned his plastic fork to his meal.

Alexis returned to her own meal but felt encroached upon and uncomfortable. "Go find another seat, please."

"Okay," Eddy agreed promptly, and slid his tray over two more spots to the end of the table.

"Why are you so stubborn and persistent?" Alexis asked forcefully in a whispering voice. "I told you how I feel."

"I'm sorry, I couldn't hear you," Eddy said, withholding all expression out of respect.

"I asked—" Alexis started but interrupted herself with her own frustration. "Why don't you just leave me alone with my feelings instead of teasing me day after day?" Alexis rephrased, having moved over three stools toward Eddy.

"I have a theory. Do you want to hear it?" Eddy asked, and he held his food in his hand, waiting for Alexis to answer.

"Not really, but yes," Alexis said, caving in while avoiding eye contact.

"I think...I think that one day in the next five years, you're going to have an awesome special friend or relationship, and then something's going to cause you to split up. And you're not going to want to call your parents or your sister when it happens, but you'll want somebody to talk to or to have lunch with...or to just be with for a while. A friend. And I think it's possible to have that type of friendship...with Alexis."

"You know it'd be more normal for my platonic friends to be girls," Alexis rationalized, picking out another disagreeable tomato from her salad.

"Normal. Okay, I'll give you that, but can a guy that you haven't kissed be platonic?"

"That all depends on his behavior," Alexis remarked.

"Hi, Eddy!" Melanie said, trying to hide the fact that her heart was racing over Eddy's choice of seats.

"Mel, you got out early. Hey, this is my friend, Alexis. Alexis, this is my girlfriend, Mel. Hey, Mel, take a seat," Eddy invited.

Not seeing enough room to sit between the seated couple, Melanie sat next to Alexis and leaned forward to make eye contact with Eddy. Eddy looked back at her inquisitiveness and gulped down his brief smile with his food.

With one hand still on her heart's fire alarm and her cheek propped up with her other, Melanie started looking diagnostically at Alexis. Not detecting any sign of smoke, Melanie's foot started wiggling with nervous energy, and she shifted her critical eyes to Eddy. If Melanie's heart had a voice, both Eddy and Alexis would not have enjoyed its shrill and heated argument, but after licking and rolling her lips between her teeth, Mel chose to say, "Alexis, you have got to tell me what color you've dyed your hair."

"There's no coloring in it," Alexis said, wanting to be offended.

"You've got to be kidding. It's real?" Melanie praised with disbelief and offloaded her bag to the floor in a more friendly manner.

"Real," Alexis promised unenthusiastically, but then her face hinted that she liked the inferred compliment.

"I hate my real hair color," Melanie admitted, an admission which peaked Eddy's interest.

"What's your natural color?"

"Nothing; there's no bold, or vibrant hues like yours. It's like a dusty flat brown," Melanie admitted and felt victorious when Eddy's eyes caught hers.

"Where'd you get your shirt? It's pretty," Alexis said, trying to be complimentary in light of Melanie's insult to her present waves of enviable golden hair.

"Oh, it's from a second-hand store. I practically have to beg my dad to let me go into a department store to dream once in a while. And all the things there end up at the second-hand stores anyway, like this piece," Melanie said and defended her disclosure. "Plus, it was only a buck-fifty."

Alexis was still hard to read but was finally showing a more pleasant expression.

"Do you want to go there to try on clothes sometime? With me?" Melanie asked hopefully.

"Why?" Alexis asked and saw from Melanie's reaction that her blunt response had been too harsh.

"Well, my dad loathes watching me try on clothes, and I'm sure Eddy has some video game he'd rather be playing. And trying on clothes is just plain-Jane boring by yourself."

"Don't you have like a myriad of other friends to go have fun with?" Alexis asked, digging to find out why Eddy's girlfriend would target her.

"Ha, my old friends. Come to find out, my *friends* were more friends with Scott than friends with me. Scott and I broke up."

Alexis felt horrible and again wondered where she acquired her talent for sparking emotional forest fires. This wondering created an uncomfortable lull while she took her few last bites. "You know what I can't figure out," Alexis said, turning onto the prospect of friendship, "I don't know how in the world you get your makeup on so perfectly every day. Every day I see you walking into school, it's like your face is glowing and so attractive."

"That's my next favorite thing to do at the department store," Melanie said, jumping on board after interrupting her wonderful exchange of subtle flirtations with Eddy.

"Yeah?"

"We gotta go sometime!" Melanie rehashed.

"We gotta go to class too!" Eddy interjected.

"Does Eddy have your number?"

"No. Well, yes. I texted him once last week when he disappeared from school after something I said," Alexis confessed. "So he probably does, but we're just lunch and math buddies."

"Can I get it from you?" Melanie asked, internalizing Alexis's confession while acknowledging the emptying cafeteria with a swing of her smooth chin.

"Here, I'll get this for you," Eddy said, taking Alexis's finished tray and disposing of the items as the girls exchanged digits.

When the three students joined the last of the line exiting the cafeteria, Eddy made sure Melanie was between him and Alexis. Situated as such, upon exiting the large space, he saw Scott and two of his well-built friends emerge from the dirtiest men's room under the central stairs of the school. Each of the three boys eyed their trio separately as they ascended the steps in procession.

After both of the parties had long ascended out of view and the central stairs had emptied of its student traffic, Charles emerged from the same bathroom shivering with energy. Looking back and forth at the vertical crossroads of the building, he decided on the up direction and leaped up the staircase toward the main lobby located one story above him. Stopping his momentum with a flat-footed slide into the lobby, he caught sight of Eddy before he disappeared through the door of his health class. "Eddy!" Charles yelled.

Eddy spun around and saw Charles approaching, but he tapped his wrist like it was a watch when he heard the tardy bell and saw Steven Kloomsfield eyeing the classroom door from his desk.

Charles was unconcerned with his own less than perfect tardy record but was intensely concerned about the plot that he was sure he had overheard from his graffitied bathroom stall. "Oh, what do I do?" Charles debated frightfully, pinioning on his feet to see an empty hallway in both directions. Thinking like a hungry fox, he dove into his bookbag and pulled out an expired hallway pass. It was a simple forgery to perform, adding Eddy's name and changing the date. Then walking to Mr. Kloomsfield's classroom as a typical office runner would, he dropped his bag a few steps away to make himself look more official. The charade was fairly easy to pull off, especially since every teacher knew that Eddy basically had a blanket excuse to leave class.

"Mr. Kloomsfield, Eddy has a phone call waiting for him in the office," Charles informed after knocking loudly twice.

"Does he need all his stuff?" Steven queried, walking over and looking at Charles more than at the office pass.

"A what? Uh, no. No, I don't think so."

"Eddy, you have a phone call in the office. Hurry back, please," Steven relayed.

Eddy initially looked both worried and confused like the two emotions had splashed from a blender onto his face, and without hesitation, he hopped out of his seat beside Melanie at the middle-ground table and out of the classroom. Completely taken by the deception, he hurried past Charles, who felt obligated to stay behind and wave awkwardly to the teacher. When the health-class door had closed and he had vacated its thin window, Charles stopped Eddy's progress with a harsh whisper and a few athletic steps.

"What's going on, Charles?" Eddy asked.

"You don't have a phone call, but I need to tell you something."

"Gentlemen, where are you supposed to be?" a voice came from an approaching hall monitor.

"We're heading to the office, Mrs. Lockingham," Eddy said.

"Well, be getting that way then."

"Yes, ma'am," the duo unanimously agreed and turned to comply.

"Get to it!" Eddy said without tilting his ear.

"I was in the bathroom taking a dump, and it took a much longer time than usual."

"Charles, that's TMI; get on with it."

Stuttering, Charles continued, "A couple of guys came in and started talking about you and how they're going to nail you after school somewhere."

"Was it Scott?" Eddy asked, correlating the group he'd seen emerge from one of the bathrooms after lunch.

"I don't know, but they sounded serious. I was holding my feet up and my poop in, and they were only going pee."

"Hello, Eddy and Charles. May I help you boys?" the secretary asked as the two boys returned to their charade upon entering the open office door.

"Um, my mom said she would call if her plans ever changed. Did she call by chance?"

"No, she did not, but we'll surely send a message with our hallway runner if she does. May I have your hall pass?" the secretary asked, reaching her hand over the counter for the standard transaction.

Charles looked blatantly at Eddy, who patted his pockets while trying to decide whether he wanted to risk handing the forged pass over.

"Oh, here it is," Eddy succumbed and handed it to the secretary. Both boys turned to leave.

"Gentlemen," the secretary said, stopping the boys in their tracks.

Eddy turned with a guilty look on his face but saw the secretary extending the same pass back over the counter.

"Thank you," Eddy said, taking the re-signed slip.

The duo left the office.

"Hey, take this," Eddy said. "Feel free to say that I needed your emotional support for a minute."

"What are you going to do?" Charles inquired, ready to split toward his own classroom.

"I'll talk to Melanie. It's probably nothing, but one can't be too careful. Thanks, Charles," Eddy said and hurried back to his classroom before he could be caught traveling the halls without permission.

"Is everything okay?" Melanie whispered in Eddy's ear once he had resettled himself in class.

"I think so; nothing to worry about," Eddy said, feeling Melanie's hand flip over to grab his under the circular table.

Eddy saw that Scott looked calm enough as the lecture continued. Then as the lecture droned on, he checked again but noted nothing strange—other than maybe his stoic posture and his appearance of paying attention.

"What was the call about?" Melanie asked, having thought through all the possibilities over the family-planning hour.

"Charles, the conniving fellow that he is, made the phone call up, so he could talk to me," Eddy said comfortably, grabbing Melanie's hand to lead her out of the classroom.

"Oh, and here I was worrying for an hour that something worse happened to your family!" Melanie relieved, putting her other hand around Eddy's arm. "What did he have to say?"

"Not much, but that he overheard a group of guys saying they were out to nail me after school today."

"Uh what!? I'd think you need to tell somebody, wouldn't you?" Melanie asked but easily read the unwillingness in Eddy's eyes. "No, like I'm telling you to tell the office, or I'm telling them for you."

"How about going together," Eddy suggested, thankful for Melanie's boldness, and he diverted their course to the nearby office across from the illuminated school library.

"Okay, here we conveniently are," Melanie said, taking the initiative to open the office door for Eddy.

"Hello, may I help you two?" the same secretary asked, lending the pair half of her attention.

"Yes, we'd—"

"I'd like to speak to a counselor," Eddy interrupted Melanie.

"Both of you together, or just you, Eddy?" the secretary asked, taking her hand off the computer keyboard and placing it on the telephone.

"Do you want to be late for class twice?" Eddy asked, letting go of Melanie's tense fingers.

"She won't be counted late, Eddy. I'll make sure of that," the secretary announced, overhearing Eddy's concern.

"I'll stay then."

"Very well," the secretary said. "Take a seat, and I'll give the counselor a call."

"I do like your T-shirt," Eddy said, complimenting Melanie as they sat down in two of the red office chairs. "It goes well with your beach jeans," Eddy continued, proving he had no fashion sense, yet he knew that he liked how the whiteness of the cotton highlighted her skin tone.

"Oh, it's just plain...beach jeans? You mean Daisy Dukes! Yeah. Again, they're second-hand material, or repurposed actually, made from my old plain-Jane throw away jeans."

"They're not plain on you though," Eddy countered. "May I use the term sexy?" Eddy asked, searching for approval after having digested that morning's conversation a hundred times in his head.

"I'd prefer the term pretty or beautiful. Or you're creative enough to make me feel attractive," Melanie encouraged honestly.

"Eddy and Miss Westin, come on in. It's Melanie, correct?" the counselor interrupted, stepping out of his office to humbly address his next students.

"Or Mel," Melanie answered as she stepped ahead of Eddy into the office.

"What can I do for you, Mel and Eddy?" the counselor, a man confident enough to wear a checkered green and pink tie in a high school, asked as they all sat down in the available seats on either side of the administrative desk.

"Well, I've heard a rumor that I feel is substantial, but I don't know how to go about verifying it or what the best thing to do about it is," Eddy started, looking to assess the counselor's level of interest.

"Please share it with me, and I'll do my best to steer you down the right road," the counselor invited, leaning back in his professional chair.

"Charles, a good friend of mine, overheard a group of boys in the bathroom after lunch that seemed serious about *nailing* me after school."

"Any guesses as to their names?"

"No, sir. This was all from Charles, who said he heard something. Can you see my predicament?" Eddy asked, looking for sympathy on the counselor's face. "Now there is a thing going on between Scott Ardan and Melanie and me—"

"I'm aware of it. He knocked over some tables this morning," the counselor admitted, tapping his fingers together.

"Do you have any suggestions?" Eddy asked when the counselor neglected to expound.

"Umm. Stick together as much as you can. Avoid Scott if you think it's him. Keep your phone handy," the counselor brainstormed out loud. "Like you said, Eddy, that sounds like a sticky one because you don't want to make relations worse, but you don't want to open yourself heedlessly to danger either. Do you guys walk home or take the bus?" the counselor asked.

"We usually walk."

"Well, today might be a good day to take the bus," the counselor proposed optimistically. "That's all I can think of to recommend until you have something more substantial, like a threatening text or voicemail. Okay?"

"Thank you," Eddy said ready to be finished.

"Here, I'll give you guys hall passes, so you're not counted tardy," the counselor offered.

"I'm meeting you out front to ride the bus home today," Melanie said, verbalizing the obvious plan as they maneuvered around the front office counter.

"I won't leave without you...and right outside the lobby," Eddy responded and pointed to the front doors of the school.

"You're taking my bus, right?" Melanie clarified, trying to loosen the tension that had raised her shoulders an inch over the duration of the interview.

"Only if you need an escort or a study buddy," Eddy said and saw a provoking smile flash under Melanie's wave of hair as they parted in the hallway.

Chapter Eleven

Melanie was lost in her thoughts during the closing stretch of her literature class, thinking about what her dad might say when he came home to find her studying with the boy she had told him about the night before. Into the thick of this pleasant reverie came a double tap on the door. A hall runner handed the teacher a note, and after glancing at the note, the teacher looked observantly at the clock and then at Melanie. Leaving mystery to mystery as to why this summons would arrive minutes before the last school bell, the teacher announced, "Melanie, you have an early dismissal; get your things."

"Really?" Melanie asked, her thoughts gathering and then scattering like a school of fish. "Okay," she acknowledged before the teacher could notice her quizzical brow, and she pulled her phone out of her bag.

"Put your phone away, Miss Westin. You won't need it for the next five minutes," the teacher instructed.

"Yes, ma'am," she said compliantly and walked out of the room to head to the office.

Once she arrived at the office, the secretary took her note and said, "Your father called and said that he needs to pick you up and that he thought he might lose you in the mess of the dismissal if he didn't get you a few minutes early."

"He wasn't kidding about a few, was he. Did he say why?" Melanie asked, imagining that the secretary's answer would be a vapor-cooling fan for her sweating curiosity.

"He didn't, but he did say that he would pick you up out front of the school," the secretary replied. Her lack of sentiment stirred worry into Melanie's private pool of thoughts.

"May I call him now?" Melanie asked as her wonder sent a cold shiver through her shoulders.

"Of course, darling."

Melanie started texting her father and saw through the office window a car pulling up to the pickup lane. Connecting the dots, she cleared out her text and started texting Eddy as she stepped out of the office door. She was blind to him at first, but the moment the office door was closed, Scott grabbed her by the arm.

"Come with me," Scott invited, forcing Melanie forward across the hall and into the vacant library. Pulling Melanie inside, he let her go and locked both doors behind him.

"Yeesh, Scott. When will you learn that pinching and grabbing someone actually hurts?" Melanie scolded as Scott continued to march her around the corner until they were out of view of the library's front windows. "You don't have to be so gruff!" Melanie reiterated with annoyance, trying to recall the thought of a cool breeze again as her heart started running wild with heat.

"That's not how it's done, Scott," Melanie objected to Scott's kiss after she had pushed and slapped him as hard as she could. She would have straightway left the library if Scott's controlling hand had released its clutch.

"I thought you'd say that," Scott said as two of his friends climbed into the library through a high window.

Melanie's heart exploded as she could see what was about to happen. "What are you going to do?" Melanie charged, her voice riddled with the toxic blend of anger, anxiety, and worry. This equated to what most would say sounded like sarcasm, and trying to play it cool, she yielded to Scott's disagreeable hands.

The final bell rang to dismiss the students when Scott answered, "You'll see. Don't move."

"What are you—" Melanie repeated as a piece of duct tape unpredictably floated down from behind her head and shut her mouth.

"I'm making you a porn star, so every guy in school can undress you when he wants," Scott said, looking up at his friend who was already holding a camera in position.

Realizing this, Melanie started to resist violently, but the other boy picked her up from behind and pinned her shoulders down to a library table. At the peak of her resistance, she walloped Scott in the stomach with her two-inch heels.

"That's okay, Mel. Everybody likes a little fight in their girl, but now it's time for me to have my fun," Scott said as he brandished a knife to aid in the removal of Melanie's inconvenient wardrobe.

--- *Less than five minutes later, chaos led a charge through the school hallways.*

Steven Kloomsfield efficiently stepped out of his classroom, ready with the stack of papers he needed copied. Walking amidst the swarming of students, he noticed the library doors oddly closed, and he stopped for a moment of consideration before continuing the few remaining steps to the office to accomplish his daily copying mission.

From a different hallway, Eddy had left his classroom with the masses and had deposited his extra books into his locker. Slamming the sheet-metal door closed in characteristic fashion, he had proceeded with the flow of students outside to figure out which of the buses would stop off near Melanie's house. Having inevitable success in locating the bus in the many-bus lineup, he returned to their arranged rendezvous at the top of the school steps and kept a keen eye out for Melanie. Eddy surveyed the students that flowed like storm water out of the school and into the bus loop and kept expecting Melanie to appear in the student tributary like a floating swan. A few false swans did float into his view, but his Melanie was absent. Agitated from waiting and feeling like he was standing in rising water from the raucous around him, he took a deep breath and kept eagerly looking for Melanie's shimmering head of hair and fashionable, white cotton T-shirt. With bus departure time approaching and tidal concerns still rising, he decided to look inside the lobby and took out his phone to check for any texts.

"You getting a ride home today?" Steven Kloomsfield asked as he stepped out of the office with his copies in hand.

"Nope, I'm waiting for Melanie," Eddy explained in brief, "We're taking the bus home."

"Yeah, I saw you two," Steven said with inference and returned his attention to his stack of papers that were uniformly divided among his fingers.

"Yeah," Eddy acknowledged, looking equally distracted at his phone.

"You'd best treat her like a queen."

"I will," Eddy automatically replied as he shot off a text to Melanie, asking her of her whereabouts.

The buses departed on schedule, and Eddy's worries swelled in his temples like fish-gills out of water. He stepped inside the office and combatively told the secretary, "Melanie Westin was supposed to meet me here ten minutes ago. Do you know anything?"

"Melanie Westin's dad picked her up about two minutes before school got out," the secretary said soothingly to counter Eddy's aggressive tone.

"Thanks," Eddy said apologetically, realizing his tenseness but still not believing Melanie would forget to text.

--- *Meanwhile under the rash blur, Melanie unsuccessfully screamed a final time.*

Melanie stopped struggling after the first of the five, hour-long minutes of abuse. All of the boyish laughing and inbred encouragement gradually fell foreign to her ears and eventually disappeared out the high window from whence Scott's two friends had arrived. Her head hurt, her foot was bleeding, her flesh felt like it was torn, and her chest still stung from Scott's hateful hands. She felt dead. Not angry, not afraid, she just felt like she had died and had been laid to rest there in the school library for all to see. She lay there mostly naked looking at tear-blurred tables and even blurrier walls of books. Eventually, feeling returned to her lifeless extremities, and she groaned under her tears, admitting to herself that she had survived and would have to do something. Haltingly, she pulled the tape off her mouth and resurrected her bleeding foot in agony. Then after screaming without a voice, she rolled off the table and suffered through the tenderness of her bruises as she searched for her backpack. Her backpack was a toss from the torture platform, and she had her phone in her shaking hand before long. Crawling herself into an aisle of books and finding support against the first dividing column, she curled up with her bag to hide the greater part of her exposed skin.

"Hi!" Eddy exasperated into the phone. Standing fifteen feet away from his girlfriend in the center of the lobby.

"Hi."

"Mel?" Eddy asked oddly, pressing his ear into the speaker.

"Yes? Hey, you don't by chance want to lend me your pants, do you?" Melanie asked, thinking of her pressing need and not of how ridiculous it would sound.

"They're yours in a heartbeat; where should I deliver them? And what happened to yours?" Eddy asked, imagining Melanie hiding from embarrassment in one of the bathrooms with a rip in her crotch.

"Scott...just cut mine off me, and I'd say from a look at them right now that they wouldn't pass the school's dress code," Melanie said though her voice broke down at the end of her confession.

Eddy's heart got shot with a swirling bullet of adrenaline. "Where are you?!?"

"The school library," Melanie answered simply enough and heard the locked library doors slam back and forth before she could add any more detail. "You found me."

"The doors are locked! Hang on!" Eddy said, trying to decide on his next move with a whip of his head up and down the hallway.

"There's a window that's open from the back if you can get to it," Melanie said softly with the clear window of escape not so clear in her blurry eyes.

"I know which one you're talking about, I'll be there in a minute," Eddy promised, bolting down the hallway to the building's nearest exit to get to the back of the library. At full sprint he caught Steven Kloomsfield by the shoulder as his teacher stepped out of his classroom for the second time.

"Woah, slow down," Steven commanded, not having time to see who clipped him.

Eddy caught his balance without losing much momentum, and yelled, "Melanie's locked in the library, and she's bleeding!" Without turning again, he slammed through the exit and out of sight. Eddy had heard Melanie say *cut* and *Scott* in the same sentence and assumed the worst.

Steven looked the other way down the hallway, and connecting his own dots, he little by little accelerated to a jog until he reached the library doors. They were indeed locked, and he dropped his briefcase there and hurried to the office to find a way inside.

Eddy saw the open window that Melanie had mentioned as he rounded the back of the brick school, and with one small jump, he was able to catch the bottom ledge and pull himself up the rough brown wall with his feet and arms. Flopping over the wide gap, he landed as carefully as he could manage. It would have been a great landing, but his backpack pulled him down onto his butt.

"Impressive," Eddy heard, and he looked toward the sound to find Melanie kiddie-corner him, leaning curled up against a column between two of the many bookcases.

"Mel!" Eddy said sympathetically, scurrying to get his shoes and pants off. "What happened?"

"I'd say that's obvious," Melanie said dryly, but the tough act melted away like snow in July. "My whole-body hurts, Eddy. And they put it all on video," Melanie admitted and looked up to find Eddy's trembling hands offering her his pants. Melanie tried to work the pants onto her legs alone, but when the door handles to the library started wiggling, Eddy scooted closer to help her finish.

"I'm going to carry you out of here. Okay?" Eddy announced.

"And where are you going to take me?" Melanie said, wanting to escape the bloody canvass of her mind.

"Wherever you want to go," Eddy replied, propping himself up by his knees.

"Well take me home then," Melanie requested and relaxed her head against the wall.

"I was thinking that you would be more interested in someplace like a hospital," Eddy suggested, readying himself to lift Melanie off the floor. "Let's take a vote. Put your hands up, if you want to go to the hospital," Eddy instructed right before Melanie reached up to lay her hands around his neck. "So, that's two in favor and zero against. Great, up we go!"

"Thank you, Eddy," Melanie said with a shallow grin as she hovered over the floor.

Eddy moved along the side of the tables, successfully getting to the door without inflicting any more trauma to Melanie's appendages. In view, his teacher stood by a janitor, who was still trying to pick from a large set of keys which would open the library door.

"Can you reach the lock, Mel?"

"If you move me closer," Melanie advised and Eddy stepped forward. "That's comfortable enough," Melanie said with a wimpy smirk.

"Why don't you carry her to the office!"

"No, why don't you just carry her outside, the paramedics will be here by that time anyway!"

"What happened, Melanie? Can I get you anything?"

"Do you need help, Eddy?"

"Some pants would be nice," Eddy replied to the string of concern, and he watched the lobby doors swing open automatically by the hands of the first-responding teachers and office workers that surrounded him like a troop of voluntary soldiers on an extraction mission. Only a handful of students were left to take notice of the body of people that moved protectively down the school steps. And by the time Eddy and Melanie had reached the bottom, the paramedics had arrived as predicted. Before the medics had finished wrapping her foot, the police had shown up and the principal was sharing the information he had gleaned from the tidbits of info that Melanie had shared on their step-by-step descent to the curbside.

Shortly after the police were finished recording Melanie's and Eddy's statements, Johnny, Frank's boss at the mechanic shop, arrived in a panicking rush to drop off Melanie's panic-stricken father, who had been contacted in a cold panic by the office secretary.

Frank scoured the people until he heard his daughter say, "Dad!"

"Is she okay?" Frank asked the first wide-eyed and intimidated paramedic he encountered before he addressed his daughter.

"I'm fine."

"She appears to be fine, but due to the nature of the incident, we are going to take her in for some scans and a more private screening environment."

Frank looked at his daughter with a look that meant only one question.

Melanie nodded with a guilty lip.

"That boy?" Frank asked to be certain and saw his daughter nod again. "That boy better hope that he and I never cross paths in this life again."

"Sir, are you Melanie's father?"

"Hey, Daddy, come here closer," Melanie beckoned, not wanting to lose her father's comforting attention to the ruckus.

"Hold on, sir," Frank said to the paramedic as he swung back to his daughter's side.

"You said you wanted me to include my boyfriend in our affairs. Well, this is Eddy Kraft, the nice one," Melanie introduced.

"Frank Westin, and where are your pants, boy?"

Eddy was unnerved enough by Frank's handshake alone, but the reminder of his pants ensured that Eddy's tongue was tied.

"On me, Daddy! He's the one that climbed through the window, let me borrow his jeans, and carried me out here to safety," Melanie facilitated happily, glad for a distraction from the event, however little it was.

"Well, then I owe you a giant debt of gratitude, Eddy Kraft. Thank you."

"And thank you for letting me befriend your daughter, sir," Eddy said, progressively overcoming his fear.

"Sir, will you be riding with your daughter to the hospital?"

"Yes, sir," Frank answered, and turned to Eddy. "Are you coming, son?"

"I'm sorry, sir. We're a crew of three today and only have one ride-along seat."

Frank's embarrassed glance was the only apology he gave Eddy.

"Don't forget to check riding in an ambulance off your bucket list," Eddy said as he watched the paramedic close the father and daughter into the backside of the vehicle.

While the ambulance motored away, the policemen followed the rest of the school workers, specifically the principle, inside, leaving Eddy alone with the two police cars and their flashing lights. From behind the lights, Steven Kloomsfield jogged up to where Eddy was standing forlornly. Impressively, Steven had covered nearly two miles from the time he had set out for the spare pair of pants—the ones that Eddy had requested—to the

time he had found and delivered them. "You wouldn't believe
how rare and protected this commodity is in our school," Steven
quipped, holding out a pair of blue basketball shorts for Eddy to
put on. "Just drop them off in class, and I'll make sure they get
back to where they belong."

"Thank you," Eddy said, still partly in his daze. After he had
put the pants on, he returned to the library and collected his and
Melanie's backpacks and things. Then before he left the
premises, he stored Melanie's bag and the extra books he would
no longer be studying that night in his locker.

--- *Great Gravitations: Journal page eighty-one, written from a solid
wood library chair while I tried to wrap my head around what had just
happened.*

Wow. I'm winded, and I'm tempted to say that girls are a lot
of work! But how could I call that work? At least when I met
Melanie's dad, I had some reputable feat to show for my
existence on this planet. I don't have a job, I don't have a car,
nor do I have a stellar educational record. Can you imagine
walking up to that size of man and saying, "Sir, here's my report
card, I did exceptionally well in Spanish this year. May I take
your daughter out on a date, please?" I really don't know how I
would have fared without Melanie there and without her perfect
introduction.

Chapter Twelve

Eddy's daze lessened to some extent as he started walking home, and he stopped to debate his destination when he reached the fork between his neighborhood and the local hospital. The hospital would be at least a forty-five-minute walk one way, which seemed relatively reasonable for walking, and home would be home, where his aunt or both his aunt and mom were probably working. After debating the two directions like a thinking statue, he decided that the likelihood of seeing Melanie once he arrived was probably little and would probably look a little weird to Mr. Westin too, so he pulled out his phone to text Kristy that he was coming home. Though the shocking part of his daze had passed, his puzzled mind still shaded his attention. His travel time crawled by like a laden locomotive, unlike if Melanie were there swinging his arm, but he eventually made it to the convenience store. Puffing out a long billow of smoke from his long train of thought, he waited for the crosswalk signal. Again puffing, he passed the postal service office and its drop boxes. After more puffs, he took a meandering left turn to arrive in his neighborhood. Eddy's heart rate had finally slowed down, and he was at the point of his walk where he would usually look in Alexis's front window to see if she happened to be in view. At first, the window was empty, but then thinking he saw movement inside, he slowed, stretching his neck backward for the chance she would appear. What he missed while he was looking was Scott stepping out in front of him from behind the large oak tree beyond Alexis's house, and that cost him a good ten steps of protective distance. Scott was hardly as intimidating as Melanie's dad but was still intimidating for a high schooler, and Eddy's feet hiccupped, stopped, and instinctively reversed course when he finally saw Scott marching toward him. Rapidly the daze and puzzlement vanished as Scott's two accomplices pincered him from his backpedaling direction. Eddy's feet again stopped him, this time in his tracks like a tree inopportunely freezing during a windy ice storm.

Scott took advantage of Eddy's fright by closing the distance faster than a renegade car on the highway, and he put him into a headlock. "How's it going now, Eddy?" Scott greeted, proud of his advantage.

"How's it going, Scott?" Eddy asked, prying at Scott's forearms to free his throat. "Why'd you—"

"What? I can't hear you. Punch him, and maybe he'll speak up," Scott commanded after he had intentionally tightened his grip and had looked around to make sure all the sidewalks were clear.

"Why'd you rape, Mel?" Eddy forced in pain, pushing air over his vocal cords through his clenched teeth.

"I have no idea what you're talking about. The only thing I know is that I'm about to nail you in the balls like you deserve," Scott said and threw Eddy into the arms of his friends. His friends easily flipped Eddy over and held him up by his armpits and elbows.

"She's at the hospital now undergoing a rape test; they're bound to find your DNA," Eddy informed, unprepared for the sharpness of Scott's punishing knee.

"We've had sex a lot, and they're bound to find your DNA too, stupid," Scott said and seemed to find pleasure in Eddy's groan. "Now that that's out of the way, why don't we see if I can bend your face into a little better shape."

"What about the video? It puts all three of you there, or maybe juvey's a place to hang out these days," Eddy said, wildly hoping that a counterstrike of reality would demobilize his assailants.

Scott punched Eddy in the face but missed his mark. "Jake deleted the video already. Right, Jake?"

Eddy tasted a mix of victory and blood in his mouth but involuntarily coughed colored spit out onto the ground toward Scott. Rebelliously, his lungs screamed for air like a clogged organ pipe.

"My face is up here, stupid," Scott said and spit with equal contempt on Eddy's hanging head.

"Tell your mom to have fun washing that out of your shoes," Eddy muttered, finding the stray thought funny enough to share after sucking oxygen in and out of his teeth to manage the pain.

"Shut up," Scott said, and he wound up his arm, aiming to hit his mark on his second throw. The blow knocked Eddy out cold.

"Watch out, Scott. A midget's about to attack you," Scott heard and thought his friend's compliment was strange in response to his consequential knuckle sandwich. Confused, Scott snorted like a college frat leader about to be pranked, and he turned, not knowing what to expect.

Reactively, Scott curled his arm to punch his way out of the surprise attack which was an easy invitation for the short attacker to lay Scott down hard onto the cement. Here, two things temporarily worked in the small and agile girl's favor. One was that the cement was a whole lot more punishing than her sparing floor, which stunned Scott worse than a stun gun would have, and two was that the other gang members were still holding onto Eddy. This meant the trained fighter had no problem knocking one of the two aggressors to his knees with a bullseye flying roundhouse kick, which left her, her being Alexis, only one athlete to fight for the next three terrorizing combinations. Ego fighters are slow, so the second take down for Alexis with her bouncing heels and swinging ponytail was as easy as pecan pie. But after that thud on the ground the number of fists doubled and then tripled, and when all three aggravated boys rushed her like they would a quarterback, they easily toppled her backward to the grass. Scott ended up on top of the pile and his two henchmen clambered back to their feet on both sides of their tackle.

Even still, a street fight is never fair and rarely ever finished after a takedown. For Alexis's sake, the ground, even with a grass cushion, makes for an unforgiving target to punch, which the biggest tackler did amidst his first few swings at the brave and evasive girl. Also, since the main gang member was unwilling to risk sacrificing his random positioning on top of the pin, the girl underneath had space to continue fighting. One timely move with her foot and the guy to her right was left with an injured knee and came down hard on his elbow. Sharply, three loud punches were sent with her strong arm, and her final one caught Scott in the throat as he clambered forward. Then with her left leg pinned anew by Scott's fallen weight, she rolled to her side and took a painful kick to the stomach, but in trapping the third assailant's foot along with her skillful twist, she made the guy to her left also crumble to the grass. She had been unbelievably fast with her attacks, but she was too disadvantaged. From her rolling maneuver, Scott finally succeeded in climbing forward, and he powerfully landed his flexed forearm on the girl's shoulder blade, rendering her immobile. Yanking up her head with a fistful of her dark hair, he seethed, "You look familiar."

"And you're more than familiar, jerk," Alexis scoffed, suffering through the pain that resonated through her scalp.

"We're going to leave now," Scott said hoarsely, pressing Alexis's head down to the grass before scampering away to ensure he avoided taking any other surprise blow or kick.

Alexis moaned after she had let a good ten waves of oxygen filter through her lungs, but when she looked and saw how Scott and his two bullyboys were running, she smiled with a twisted sense of satisfaction. Then remembering Eddy, she rolled up onto her elbow and progressively onto her knees before crawling over to tend to him.

"Hi," Alexis greeted.

"Hi," Eddy said as the world came into focus, not recognizing the tender voice that greeted him.

"Can you get up?" Alexis asked, seeing the discolored skin around Eddy's left temple.

"I don't know. Should I try?" Eddy asked, pressing the side of his head as Alexis's dirty-smeared face came further into focus. "It looks like they got you too. Did you do your judo on them?" Eddy asked, feeling a weird boost of energy tickling his jaw after he identified the pretty frame of his friend's face that looked like a freckled wildflower scuffed with chocolate.

Realizing she could probably make up whatever story she wanted, Alexis answered, "Yeah, and you should have seen them all running away, hobbling like they'd just gotten run over by a truck."

"Thank you," Eddy said, his thoughts skipping to a conclusion. "And you're not a truck, you're a Ferrari. A red-hot Ferrari."

"Yeah, if only people around here appreciated exotic sports cars as much as you do. I have to add though, to be honest, that if Scott had wanted to, he could have easily snapped my neck at the end of the fight," Alexis admitted, balancing next to Eddy in a squat. "You know, you sure aren't very resilient to punches," Alexis insulted, watching Eddy feebly prop himself up. Her shoulders shuddered in the aftermath of her adrenaline, and her following blend of emotions could have inspired a novel.

"No, I'm pretty sure that I'm allergic. What do you think?"

Alexis laughed. "If you get to your feet, I'll walk you home."

"Why no help...in getting to my feet?" Eddy asked, feeling slightly dizzy as he lifted his head off the ground.

"Because, if you can't get to your feet, I'm going to make you stay right there and call an ambulance!" Alexis said, laughing again at her need for logic.

"Good point. Okay, here it goes," Eddy warned. "How long were you fighting?"

"Oh, about a minute maybe. I can't wait to tell my instructor how big these dudes were."

"Scott's pretty big, but not as big as Melanie's dad," Eddy said, taking his first couple steps hesitantly. "I didn't know the two other guys though."

"Jake Frasier and Juan Garcia, they're both line backers. Jake called me a midget, so I kicked him first," Alexis said proudly, grabbing Eddy's arm courteously when he started swaying like his ankles thought the sidewalk was melting.

"So, you got to be a hero today. I got be a hero today. I'd say that's enough heroism for an afternoon. Don't you think?" Eddy said, wiping the side of his head again, and this time checking for blood.

"Who'd you have to battle?" Alexis asked with an equal dose of disbelief and interest.

"I had to help Melanie out of the library," Eddy said, gaining confidence on his feet again and walking a few steps with Alexis's help.

"When you put it that way, it doesn't sound like she got herself stuck."

"No, Scott did her in too," Eddy said and checked his elbow, which felt freshly skinned.

"He's more than a jerk. He should get expelled."

"Oh, he will be; I'm sure of that. Are you okay with me calling the police?" Eddy asked, his presence of mind returning to him as he looked back at Alexis's house from the ten paces or so that he had taken down the uneven sidewalk.

"Oh, I didn't know if you wanted me to or not."

"Are you sure of the names, Jake and Juan?" Eddy asked, working his phone out of his backpack.

"Positive!" Alexis said.

"Can we sit on your porch while we wait?" Eddy asked, feeling a little dizzy again and feeling Alexis stiffen her hands around his arm.

"Sure," Alexis said without leaving Eddy's side.

--- *Forty-five minutes after the fight and ten minutes after the interview with the police officers, Eddy found his way home with Alexis.*

"What in tarnation happened to you?" Cynthia asked, dropping what she was doing to come take a closer inspection of the obvious. "I was beyond worrying and to the point of calling Mel...the school to find out what was taking you so long after your text to Kristy."

"A couple of flying fists from Melanie's ex-boyfriend," Eddy downplayed.

"Well, I'm going to call the school anyway!"

"Okay, I didn't think about the school. I just finished talking to the police," Eddy informed, looking back through the front door. "Hey, Alexis, come meet my mom and Aunt Kristy," Eddy called to Alexis, who was still standing on the front porch.

Alexis stepped inside and waved like she had been invited into an away team's locker room.

"This is my friend, Alexis. Alexis, this is my mom, Cynthia, and Aunt Kristy," Eddy introduced and pointed.

"Oh dear, he got you too?" Cynthia sympathized, noticing a scrape on her jaw that had flushed a true red.

"Oh, this is nothing but something to show off to my judo instructor tomorrow," Alexis said, shying away from the attention.

"Yeah, Mom, she took on three linebackers by herself."

"And where were you?" Cynthia asked, looking for his stake in the fight.

"Well, they had already run me through," Eddy answered flatly and treated the details like they were self-explanatory.

"Well, Alexis, dinner is on the table. Would you care to join us?" Cynthia said warmly. "It's the least a mother could do to repay such fearless kindness."

"I'll have to ask," Alexis kindly replied, petting her dark hair as she answered.

--- Great Gravitations: Journal page eighty-three, written in pencil on my gray pillow that night.

I had a great time with Alexis at dinner, and my mom insisted on driving her home due to the recent events. However, after the ride, I got a little talking to again from my mom about Melanie. Nothing mean. But after my mom finished her very good reasons for demanding my abstinence, I had to do my part and confess the day's events, followed by my sexual relationship with Melanie. It wasn't comfortable, but it was honest. Do you know what my mom said? Nothing. Well, after a Red Sea crossing of silence, she asked me to continue, so I did. I told her what I was thinking and that I don't know how as a Christian you're supposed to bridge this gap between sex and marriage when marriage seems so far away and sex is right here and now. For a second time, my mother refrained from arguing, so I continued telling her my thoughts. I told her that I think it would be by sheer providence in a perfect world that both a girl and a boy happen to like each other, that both the girl and the boy happen to want to save sex for marriage, and that both the girl and the boy are even able to wait for marriage despite their good intentions. Sex is a strong feeling! Wouldn't that be nice if waiting was the norm and not the exception? Although I couldn't then and there adequately explain it to my mom, having my dad hand me that condom across the table along with the best sex and relationship advice he could give opened me up to this new and exciting world outside of pornography. Now I can finally say that I know what I want to happen when it comes to my sex life, or rather my marriage life. I know my preference and my hope. And though I don't know how the two will eventually connect, you can't yank this foundation out from under me like you could have before with a transient curiosity. This way will last longer and be truer than an adolescent's whim to *go for it.* And if all I wanted was to add *notches* to my belt, as one too many boys have said, that's just pitifulness personified. One thing I do know though, is that Melanie's dad asked me to join them for dinner after school tomorrow! Not Melanie, but her dad! Okay, Melanie probably had a lot to do with it. But wow!

--- That next morning, after Eddy had jumped up at the first buzz of his alarm, he flew through his morning routine with uncontainable energy.

Besides his walking much more alertly through his neighborhood and tripping on a few cracks, ledges, and roots that impacted the sidewalks, Eddy easily reached Melanie's house and knocked on the door. Frank answered the knock which surprised Eddy a bit.

"Hi Eddy, I heard what happened," Frank said gruffly.

"Hi."

"Melanie will be right—" Frank started to excuse, but his daughter interrupted him with a tap and push and, after nearly collapsing, ended up in Eddy's arms.

Melanie kissed Eddy for longer than she should have, making Frank shake his head and disappear into the house along with his fading instruction, "Remember you have to buy the groceries before you can make dinner tonight!"

"Who's cooking?" Eddy asked, trying to hide the fact that her kisses were quite painful.

"We are!"

After (Sex) Word

Eddy waited for another moment on Melanie's doorstep that same morning while she hopped back inside for her shoes like a girl getting ready for her sixteenth birthday party. The sky was clear, and the sun had already illuminated every corner of the yard.

Melanie came back rosy-faced and gladly put her hand in Eddy's. Then like a playground swing, they pushed off the steps after having conquered what felt like the world the day before.

By the time the couple made it to the middle of the yard, Eddy had started playing with the newly discovered ring on Melanie's finger.

"Stop it!" Melanie said with annoyance.

"Stop what?"

"Stop playing with my ring. I can't tell if you're making fun of it or just fidgeting," Melanie said self-consciously.

"Here let me see it," Eddy said, picking up Melanie's tender hand. Eddy breathed in a short breath as he made the connection from the ring to its position on her left ring finger.

Melanie was wearing her heart on her sleeve as she waited to find a reaction, any reaction, on Eddy's face. When the reaction formed, it was as confusing as she had expected. "Can you explain why...why you're frozen?" Melanie asked, her eyes finding nervous tears.

"I just talked to my mom last night about this," Eddy admitted, smiling like his cheeks were telling his forehead a secret. "And I was honest with her. I was honest about our having sex...I was honest about what I wanted verses what she wanted, and I didn't know how they were going to ever match up."

"Okay, I'm only getting half of what you're saying because I'm so scared of what I think you might say. Please tell me again," Melanie asked courageously, letting her hand stay afloat with Eddy's.

Eddy lifted Melanie's new ring to his lips to make it easier for her to understand. "What's the probability of finding a girl that wants to wait and yet wants to be a companion while you wait with her?"

"I don't know," Melanie exhaled, happily pulling her new ring with its acceptance close to her chest. "My dad has never rushed me out so quickly to buy me something so expensive before."

"You picked a good one!" Eddy complimented, letting their hands fall between them.

"It doesn't matter if I picked a good ring. I still have to pick a patient guy, and that patient guy has to want to wait for me," Melanie said, progressing down the sidewalk at her ginger pace like the houses were carnival booths and they were enjoying the atmosphere of the county fair.

"I don't know about you, but my mind's about to explode," Eddy said conclusively. "With joy!"

Melanie just bit her lower lip, looking secretly for any sign of hidden resentment. After looking again and again as the conversation ebbed and flowed, they finally made it to the yard with the half-wall, and Melanie was convinced.

"What do you say we sit for a bit here before we go show off your ring and change tables in health class? I bet people are going to be so confused," Eddy said and felt like he had to explain. "You're wearing a purity ring, the entire school knows we've had sex, and we're still dating. Kind of backwards, right?"

"I know, but you see it too, right?"

"See what?" Eddy asked unsure of what she would add, and he stopped to help Melanie down to a flatter spot on the wall.

"You see that I couldn't have had enough sex with Scott to keep his interest, but in seeing how amazing it can be with the right person, I...I regret that I didn't save it for the right person. Is this comfortable?" Melanie asked sincerely when she had placed her head on Eddy's shoulder.

"Totally comfortable."

--- *Great Gravitations: Journal page ninety-nine, written after shopping with Melanie, after cooking with Melanie, and after eating with her and her father, who still kind of scares me because he talks like rocks are in his throat.*

You know, I came home from school with an inkling to read the *Song of Songs*. I felt like there must have been something I missed when I read it the first four times. Honestly, the fifth time didn't help much more, other than bringing to light some analogies that I've now experienced with Melanie. "For love is strong as death; jealousy is cruel as the grave." That's true. I asked my mom for help with the passage, and she told me to study it like I would study a poem written to me by Melanie. I guess that puts it into perspective, seeing that it's rather artistic and has guided hundreds of thousands of people through the unknown beginnings of their sexuality. Maybe it's like my dad said, me asking the girl for directions, except this is the God of Abraham giving his directions. Either way, I'll have another stab at it tomorrow during Melanie's volleyball practice if she goes, and maybe it will start connecting the dots for me like it has for so many other people over the past almost 3000 years.

--- *Great Gravitations: Journal page one hundred seven, after agreeing with Melanie that studying alone together at her house before her dad got home was a bad idea.*

I wouldn't say that I've had any major revelations about *Song of Songs*, but I do find it odd that Solomon doesn't call his lover by name. I wonder if that means he intends his writing to be poetry and his lover is fictional, or maybe that this is his wisdom, compiling all the experiences that he had from all his lovers into one piece. Or maybe this is a diary of sorts, and he just doesn't know the girl's name yet, so he's describing how love should be. "Awaken not my love until he pleases." I could see this making sense, Solomon writing this love letter as an outlet, addressing his future bride that he hasn't met yet, or that he has met, but the time for consummate marriage is still far off in the future. Maybe that's how he handled this gap between adolescence and marriage, with nameless love letters.

It hit me on my walk home, before diving again into this puzzling poem, that maybe Melanie Westin and I won't end up together. I mean, what comes after sex if not a breakup or marriage, and why should I be so concerned about either, breakup or marriage, in high school?! But for real, maybe my dad put it right. Just because he put a condom on the table along with his insight doesn't mean that having sex is what's

even important. Do...what's in the best interest of the girl you're
interested in, and maybe the best thing to do is to not participate
in awakening her love until he pleases, he being her bridegroom,
like Solomon's poem says. And along those same lines, to pray
that no one else awakens yours either. So, I guess you could call
that kind of a revelation, but how do I not awaken Melanie's
love? It appears as if love is already awake, or maybe that's what
she was trying to fix when she said, "she...still has to pick a
patient guy" for the ring to work. If so, thank you, Melanie! I
want to wait and prepare for this awakening together. I'm glad
we changed tables.

A LETTER FROM THE AUTHOR

Dear Reader,

I highly respect my traditional-leaning mother, and even more so after she approached me with her first edits of this manuscript by passionately decrying, "Josiah, there's NEVER a time where it's *in a Girl's Best Interest* to have sex outside of marriage!" Her protest made my inner ligaments stretch and smile, if organs such as your heart and lungs can react as naturally as your cheeks, because I had achieved my angle of throwing this topic into the daylight which gave my heart's heavy hope a rocket booster. Nevertheless, at my mother's recommendation, I must insist that if you have reached a different conclusion after perusing my subversive tale, I beg you to take a more careful, and perhaps wider, reading of the topic before rendering judgement, or worse rendering choice. To my parent readers: Please, please, please, train up your proteges to the height of what's healthy and sacred. Then to my independent, free-thinking, truth-dreaming, packed-with-potential readers: Perhaps I could impel you with a free verse poem that's permeated with the platitude of this book—

Like a father's pride in his son's performance,
Like a smile after a kiss,
Like a golden harvest after healthy rains,
Enjoyment swells the more you plan,
The more you work,
And especially the more you've had to wait.

I hope you'll see it and mean no offense by it. I leave you now, hoping to have cuffed a few dangers that hide in history's shadows.

Sincerely,
JH

ABOUT THE AUTHOR

Josiah Hutchison was born in Michigan and attended high school in Portage. Portage was home through his teenage years and was where he began his literary pursuit by writing lyrical poetry. For the birth of his son in 2011, he self-published *The Story of a Cloud*, a children's bedtime story of a cloud racing the sun to the top of the sky. After many conversations with friends concerning the epidemic topics of the day, he set out to write the fictional story of Anna Purse. When he had finished the manuscript, now published as *The Monstrosity or Anna Purse* in 2018, Josiah set out to work on his three other topical pieces, *All in a Girl's Best Interest* being one of them. Then in 2019, he whittled his second manuscript down to its present size, hoping the story's boldness and brevity would address the missing conversation in the home and would expose the misrepresentations of sex and pornography found in the public sphere. Yet, he knows more intimately than most that intention and execution are two difficult matters to mate, and only you will be able to decide whether a sword thrust followed this matador's cape work or not.

Made in the USA
Columbia, SC
20 May 2024

35512376R00083